*S*leeping *Sisters*

Daniel Adkins

WWW.Daniel Adkins Secret Bookshelf .Com

Published in 2014 by FeedARead.com Publishing

Copyright © Daniel Adkins.

A CIP catalogue record for this title is available from the British Library.

A Note From The Author

My name is Daniel Adkins and I have lived in and around Bury St Edmunds for most of my life. The ideas for this novel have been drawn from local Suffolk ghost stories, such as the Red Barn Murders, the Witchcraft trials of Mathew Hopkins and the legends of Borley Rectory. However the story itself is a complete work of fiction from my own imagination, written mostly from the front seat of my taxi, whilst I was waiting for clients.

As a self-published author, I rely on word of mouth to publicise my work. So if you enjoy reading any of my books, then please tell all your friends. The best way to find out more about my books is to visit my website, where you can see all of my latest titles, read free samples and you can also find links to follow me on social media, so you can keep up to date with all my latest release dates…

WWW.Daniel Adkins Secret Bookshelf .Com

Contents

My Sister Sleeps   1

An Old Woman Wakes   7

Dead or Alive?   14

Racing Daylight   20

For the Love of Our Sisters   27

Locking Up and Turning Out the Lights   33

The One Eyed Monk   42

Double or Nothing   59

The Hangover from Hell   69

You Know What I am   85

Billy Has Lost the Plot   91

Goodbye Billy   106

Evelyn and Madelyn   112

The School Run of Saint Francis   123

Nowhere to Run   133

Stand and Deliver   137

Alice   150

Dead Letter   160

Paige   172

Fight For Your Sisters   188

Hope   201

Keep Your Sisters Close & Your Enemies Closer   210

– My Sister Sleeps –

Crimson leaves lie strewn across the shingle path, like blood-stained footprints leading towards a crime scene. I find myself short of breath – my feet racing to keep up with Jack's torchlight as it dances through the graveyard.

'Jack, are you sure you want to do this?' I ask.

'Come on!' he says, flinging back his hood and hurrying around the tower towards the chapel door.

Its weathered paint blisters and peels and the lock seems welded shut. Jack's knuckles turn white as he twists the iron ring. The hinges let out a high-pitched scream, but much to my surprise, the latch scrapes over the top of its hasps and the door slowly opens.

The whole place smells of damp, warmed by moonlight spraying through the stained glass windows and painting everything red. Then a howl splits the silence and a lone raven swoops down from the rafters.

'Get away from me!' I scream, holding my hands up to protect my face.

The bird sweeps past and heads straight outside – as if he'd been waiting centuries for a chance to escape. I slam the heavy door behind him and Jack bolts around too, his shoulders hunching up and swallowing his neck.

'It's all right,' he says, as much to himself as me. 'Let's get this thing over with and get out of here.'

1

We sit together in the middle of the aisle and the cold floor nibbles its way through my jeans. My eyes work their way around the room. Six rows of dust-covered pews gather either side of us, facing a wooden altar. Beyond them, ornate carvings scale the walls, leading towards six stone cherubs that sit amongst the roof beams.

'What do you make of them?' I point out one with ruby-encrusted eyes. 'They're more demonic than angelic.'

Jack glances up and nods. Then he continues emptying the contents of his satchel onto the floor. Four hessian-coloured candles in cheap iron holders, a half-empty bottle of green twenty-twenty, a crystal-cut shot glass and a rolled-up sheath of leather bound by a lacy ribbon.

'Are you sure you know what to do with all this?' I ask.

Jack takes a phone from his pocket and starts stroking the screen until a diagram appears. It casts a tender light that grazes his high cheekbones and nestles in the tangles of his spiked hair. Our eyes meet. He's far too handsome for his own good – almost pretty like a girl. Then his gaze shoots past mine and his big brown eyes roll upwards.

'Oh, I almost forgot,' he says.

'Forgot what?'

Jack pulls a silver Pandora bracelet from his pocket and places it down between us. I feel a stammer in my chest and for half a second it's like he is giving it to me.

But he's not.

Just like him, the bracelet belongs to my twin sister Scarlett. He bought it for her a couple of weeks ago, as a present for our eighteenth. But later that day there was a terrible accident, and Mum ended up giving the bracelet back to him, not forever, just for safekeeping until Scarlett wakes up.

Jack pushes aside the bracelet and unties the ribbon around the scroll. He lets it slowly unravel, revealing a sheet of coffee-coloured parchment paper, which has the alphabet scrawled across it in dark copperplate calligraphy.

He caresses its breadth, flattening its curve, before clamping the corners with the candleholders. Once it's even, I can make out an array of symbols circled around its edges and the words 'yes' and 'no' sitting boldly in the two top corners.

Jack takes a lighter from his pocket and frantically sparks at its wheel. One, two, three times he tries, but the stubborn thing won't light.

'Hold the gas on and I'll do the rest,' I say, snapping my index finger with my thumb and striking the wheel.

A tiny flame licks its way up over the silver rim and Jack looks back at me, wide-eyed, like I performed some sort of minor miracle.

'Just a little trick I learnt,' I say.

3

Jack slowly lights the candles and they cast elongated shadows that dance around us. Then he fills the shot glass with twenty-twenty and holds it up high.

'For Scarlett!' he says, knocking it back and slamming the glass upside down into the middle of the parchment paper.

We both sit still for a while. A cold shiver uses each bone in my back like a rope ladder. The amber flames of the candles spit soot as they wane and flicker. Then I place my hands on the upturned glass, waiting for Jack to rest his on top.

'I can't believe we are doing this, she isn't even dead,' I say.

But Jack's got this crazy idea that her soul might be trapped somewhere in-between.

'Is anybody there?' he says, his voice shaking.

There's a stomach-curdling silence. My pulse rebounds against the back of the glass. Then, for some reason that I can't explain, a wave of mischief passes through my fingertips.

I scrape the glass towards the word 'yes' and laugh.

Jack's eyebrows rise and the sound of a dry swallow echoes amongst the rafters.

'Don't worry, it was only me,' I say, laughing. 'It was only…'

But as the words fall out of my mouth, the shot glass starts to slide around the board. Jack flings off his hands – now only mine touch it. Faster and faster the little glass goes, hitting different letters, far too quickly for me to follow.

I try to let go – but I can't.

My head drops, my arms stretch out, my whole frame flies forward. My body no longer my own, compelled into propulsion. My free will lost, contorted into convulsions.

I breathe – I can't – I choke – I stop.

The glass stops too.

I raise my head to see Jack cowering in a heap on the floor. Then the chapel door flies open and a wild wind races in – fanning the flames of the candles three inches high. The glass starts up again, slowly, more surely, screeching across the paper like naughty fingers scraping down a blackboard.

It spells a name…

R, O, S, E

It makes no sense…

It's my name!

The flames go out and a jolt of electricity passes from my fingertips right up my back. I'm pulled to my feet and hung before Jack, who peels himself off the floor like a holy man from a prayer mat. He looks up at me – stares right through me. His girly pink skin turns a sickly shade of green and his mouth bursts open in disbelief.

I take a look behind me. There's a girl standing there, clear as day. She can't be more than sixteen – tall, blighted and painfully thin. She's dressed in dirty rags that hang in ruffles off her wasted frame. My eyes fix on her soot-stained skin, not in fear but in sympathy, as tears roll down her face and cleanse her cheeks.

'Jack, Jack. Can you see her?' I say. 'Tell me you can see her?'

Jack jumps to his feet and bolts for the door.

I want to follow, but for some reason I can't. The glass spelt out my name and the girl's hands reach out – wanting something from me.

She bends down and picks up Scarlett's bracelet, caressing it between her thumb and forefinger – dangling it between us like a peace offering.

I take a tiny step closer, with a tightness in my chest. My breathing is shallow as I reach out to touch the cold silver chain. Both of us hold on for a moment, which stretches and lingers. Then the girl's eyes turn burning red, like the demonic cherub's on the wall. Her mouth falls open and she lets out a satanic scream.

My grip fades and the bracelet falls to the floor.

I turn my back and run down the aisle, escaping through the doorway into the cold autumn night.

– An Old Woman Wakes –

I arrive home alone, tired and breathless with a tangle of auburn ringlets stuck to my cheeks and my nose leaking like a dripping tap. The light makeup I put on earlier must be smeared all over my face, and mud is splattered right up the back of my trousers and caked around the soles of my nearly-new-but-never-to-be-white-again sport shoes.

I'll kill that Jack O'Connor for leaving me like that!

Luckily Mum doesn't seem to notice my state of distress. She meets me outside amidst a wet blustery wind, car keys in hand and a frown slapped across her face. She points to her watch, wheezes a heavy sigh like she's the one who's had a bad day, and then hurries me into Bluebell – the battered hatchback that's been in our family for years.

Much to my surprise, she doesn't even tell me off as I slump into the cheap velour seat. She simply turns her head and gives me that look. The *'I'm not angry at you, but I'm disappointed'* look. Then she turns the key, along with the cold shoulder, and shuns me.

We head off in the direction of the hospital and into a deluge of sharp, slanted rain. The oncoming headlights cast golden rosettes right across the windscreen and the warmth of my body fogs the glass. A heavy pitter-patter fills the silence, so I wipe the passenger-side window clear and watch the world go by.

7

Even though Mum clearly *is* angry at me, it's not unusual for us to sit in silence on the way to visit Scarlett. To say I'm upset, or to ask Mum how she feels, is to say, or ask nothing at all. To say that Scarlett will wake up soon sounds stupidly naive. So normally silence is the order of the day, and despite the unusual events earlier, today is no different.

We twist and turn through the winding one-way streets of the medieval town, passing row after row of miserly dwellings cobbled together from the same sad flint-stone that makes up the chapel. Busying my hands through the sodden curls of my hair, I try not to think about it, but I still can't get the ghost of that girl out of my head.

Built around an abbey over a thousand years ago, I'm sure Burnham All-Saints has lots of secrets to tell about its past. But on the whole it's a miserable little place, where time seems to have stood still. Unless you're over eighty or a tourist, and then its Tuesday afternoon market, nestled on the banks of the river Bream, probably has a quaint kind of charm to it.

We stop at traffic lights on our approach to the town's picturesque main square. Victorian terraces give way to three-storey Georgian mansions, painted in pastel shades of pink and yellow. Their oversized sash windows peer out at the Norman Tower, which houses the old abbey gate. It's in a state of perfect repair, theatrically lit to show off its steel portcullis that's gaping open like an angry mouthful of teeth.

A group of girls from the lower sixth cross the road in front of us, desperately dressed in short skirts and low-cut tops. Mum flicks her eyes as they pass and I know what she's thinking before she even says a word.

'Why haven't they got coats on, they'll catch pneumonia out there,' she sighs.

'For God's sake Mum, it's not the dark ages,' I say. 'You're so embarrassing sometimes.'

I'm more interested in why they're bothering to go out at all on a Monday night. Even if they do get served, all the pubs will shut by half eleven. And even then they'll be mostly full of fat old men playing dominoes. Everybody knows you have to wait until the weekend for the town's one and only nightclub to open – if you can call it that!

It's a prefabricated building near the station, officially known as Club Brasilia's. But it's not some cool salsa club like you might find in Soho or something. It's more *Krazy-Kev's all-night disco roadshow*, playing music that was lame in the eighties, and is, well, just tragic now.

Scarlett liked to call it *Club Paedophilias*. Not just because of its rhyming qualities when you're drunk, but for the two types of people that it seems to attract – underage girls and dirty old men.

Thankfully we won't have to suffer it much longer. Both Scarlett and I have offers to go to Central Saint Martins in London next year – her to do fashion and me to do literature. My only worry is that she might not make it now. Even if she does wake up before the exams, she'll have to repeat the year for sure.

So I've already decided to take a gap-year to help her through it. There's no way on Earth I can leave her to rot here all alone. She'd rather I turned the life-support off now.

The lights are green by the time the last of the half-naked girls have made it to the other side, delaying us all of half a second. Mum lets out another long, heavy breath. But if that hadn't wound her up enough, now an old man walks out into the road, even though the lights have long since turned.

He cuts a strange sight, out at this time of night, at his age. Dressed in a top hat with torn, tattered tails, he looks like something straight out of a Dickens novel. Halloween isn't until the weekend and he isn't with a group of people in fancy dress or anything. He's in a land all of his own, seemingly oblivious to the world speeding by.

And Mum, she seems oblivious to him.

The wipers squeal across the windscreen, which has dried whilst we've been still. Our wheels spin as Bluebell lurches forward. I try to scream to tell Mum to stop, but my dry mouth chokes. It all happens too quickly. My head flies back from Mum's self-help style of driving. Our paths lock. My hands cover my eyes, scared to see the man's face when he bounces onto the bonnet.

But nothing happens.

10

I peel away my fingers and look into the frosted glass of the rear view mirror. Somehow he's completely unharmed, like he passed right through us. Then, turning around, I catch Mum's face, mute and emotionless.

I swivel back to peer out of the peephole I made on the passenger-side window. Then I flinch. My eyes are met by a horse-drawn cart, pulling alongside us at pace.

It's made from ash-coloured wood, crested in gold lettering that glints in the streetlights shining down from above. It's impossible to miss it, sitting on bright red wheels that must be twice the height of Bluebell.

'Didn't you see that, Mum?' I say, still a little breathless.

But her bloodshot eyes don't even turn in my direction, let alone behind us. She just sweeps a few strands of her greasy hair over her ear, wipes the windscreen with her soggy sleeve and keeps on going regardless.

The traffic slows to a crawl as we trundle across the central square. A sickness swells in my guts. Rather than being met with the usual midweek scene of two men walking dogs and a lonely piece of tumbleweed blowing down the street, Burnham All-Saints seems unusually alive.

Painted ladies pull up bright red dresses to advertise their wares, whilst a scrum of barrow boys brawl to be the first ones to buy. Market traders hustle and crowds bustle, as people drink and fight in a pickpocket's delight. Priests and monks hurry out of the old abbey gate and dive into the deep abyss of debauchery. Rich men, poor men, vicars and tarts, all rubbing shoulders in a multitude of sins.

I desperately try to speed us away, digging my feet so hard into the floor pan of rusty Bluebell it's a wonder they don't push through. I rub my eyes, but it makes no difference at all. Mum might not scc it and it's probably best that she doesn't in her condition, but I clearly can.

The ghostly figures swarm around our car like monkeys at a safari park. At first they seem completely unaware of us. Then there's a tap on the window. A young man in a flat-cap flashes me a smile. I hold up my hand and our fingers meet on either side of the glass. It settles my breathing and spreads a sense of calm.

I don't think he means any harm.

Then my head hits the backrest as the line of cars speeds up, leaving him trailing behind. My stomach still hasn't caught up when I'm thrown forward by Mum stabbing the brakes at the last set of traffic lights before the Humping Monks – two narrow humpback bridges that span the Bream and head out of Burnham's main square.

My eyes fix on the rear view mirror. I didn't imagine it. Sleepy Burnham really is swinging like she would have in her heyday. Then I look up. Instead of being greeted by one red light beaming down on us, I'm met by two red eyes and a girl with coal-coloured cheeks.

She places her hands on Bluebell's bonnet, like she's about to push us backwards over the bridge. Then she attacks the windscreen with a burning stare, which almost shatters the glass. The thumping returns to my chest. A cold bead of sweat runs down my spine. It's got to be the same girl that Jack and I woke in the chapel, but somehow she seems different to the others.

The lights turn green. My grip tightens around the coat hanger above the door. Mum revs the engine and drives forward.

Somehow Bluebell bounces safely over the Humping Monks, passing right through the girl. And I'm left wondering who the hell she is and what the hell she wants from me.

– Dead or Alive? –

We rattle over a minefield of potholes and finally
Bluebell comes to rest between two shiny four-wheel
drives, which have probably never been so far off-road
in their whole lives. My stomach still swirls like I've
recently got over a bout of travel sickness, and although
I'm glad to have left the haunted streets of Burnham
behind, we've just pulled into the last place you'd want
to be if you were suffering from hallucinations of the
dead.

Or, as Mum puts it, the last place you would want to
be if you were suffering from anything at all, but she's
only annoyed because nobody can seem to wake up
Scarlett.

I watch through the window as Mum shovels a
handful of coins into the parking machine and struggles
back through the rain with a ticket. Part of me wishes I
could wait in the car until visiting hours have finished,
but I know Mum would never understand, so
reluctantly I follow her up the concrete steps and walk
towards the entrance.

Suffolk General is a sad nineteen-seventies building,
flat-roofed, with rotting facia boards. A broken neon
sign buzzes above the doorway, and suddenly, it feels
like a light-bulb has been switched on in my head. If I
can just keep it together until we get to Intensive Care,
then at least I'll be able to see my sister. Now I get to
see her every night – so that in itself may not sound like

14

motivation enough to run through the corridors of the dead, the dying and the undecided. But once I get there, maybe I'll be able to see her spirit and maybe even direct it back into her body.

The automatic door swishes open; at the same moment, the sound of a siren splinters the night. An ambulance screeches to a halt behind us and two men frantically lower an elderly woman from the back. Her head pokes out from a bloodied yellow blanket and her blue-veined feet look like mouldy lumps of Stilton. She seems seriously hurt and if she's not dead already, then sadly, I think she soon will be.

The paramedics wheel her towards the door – one carries a set of defibrillators, whilst the other chats to her cheerfully, seemingly desensitised by his job toward the seriousness of her condition. 'Don't worry, you're going to be fine,' he says. 'We'll have you patched up in no time at all.'

At that moment, her ghostly spirit bolts through the covers, rolls off the side of the stretcher and runs off into the night.

I swallow a bit of sick that hits the back of my throat. It's the first time I've ever seen anyone die and it's not something I want to get used to. But worse than that, it makes me realise just how difficult this is going to be.

How the hell am I going to tell who is dead and who is alive, without looking completely crazy?

We follow the ambulance men through the automatic doors and the thick stench of institutional disinfectant wafts in the air. Much to my relief, the waiting area is surprisingly empty and the old lady is swiftly taken behind a screen of curtains.

We speed past and head up the main corridor, where a shoeless man bounds towards us. Wheeling his intravenous drip along with one hand, he's clutching at a pack of cigarettes in the other.

Alive, I think. Although he'll be lucky to make it to the morning if he doesn't lay off the extra-strong Red Stripes and have the sense to start wearing some slippers.

We continue through two doors with wire-framed windows and Mum glances back to see if I'm keeping up. She doesn't even see the candle-wielding nurse heading right for her.

Dead: *no doubting that one.*

Two lefts and a right, then we pass a well-lit courtyard, where a wooden wishing well sits amidst a pond full of water lilies. It's surrounded by beds of winter pansies, exotic grasses and long reedy cordylines. Mum says that's where the parking money goes, to keep the *Hope Gardens* full of hope. But to me it just seems like a complete waste of time and effort.

Two more rights, one more left, and we're greeted by a ginger-haired man with heavily pockmarked skin. He's of agricultural build – broad shoulders sloping towards a thick neck and giant hands perfectly formed

16

for strangling horses. 'Don't let them take me!' he shouts at the top of his voice, reaching out to me with his fat worming fingers.

Now that's a tricky one: escapee from the mental health ward or deceased axe-murder running from the hounds of hell?

I decide to do what Mum does and bow my head as we hurry past him.

Finally we arrive at Intensive Care. The woman on reception peers over the top of her trashy magazine, points at the anti-bacterial hand wash dispenser and then waves us past.

We walk down the corridor into Scarlett's ward. Six beds poke out behind wipe-clean curtains, which are so miserable they must be specially made for wards filled with unconscious people. A heavy breathing fills the air and there at the end of the line is my twin sister Scarlett, lying in the last bed by the window.

She rests peacefully, or as peacefully as you can looking like the elephant man. Her face still swollen, a large trunk-sized tube coming from the mask around her mouth and racing off into a machine that helps her breathe. A tangle of wires run around the top of her bed and eventually terminate into a green-screened monitor that beeps away slowly like a metronome.

Mum gently lifts Scarlett's thick fringe and tucks it behind her ear, whilst I stare at her, cold and still. I could never see the likeness between us until her

17

accident, but now she's lying there completely motionless it's almost like looking at my reflection.

I scan the room, past the cheap pine bedside cabinet where a wilting bunch of lilies slump in the corner. My heart begins to beat more quickly, searching for her spirit, hoping that it's sitting somewhere beside her bed. Strangely, the little green monitor seems to mimic me, too, before slowing back down, as the only 'presents' I spot are the cards and gifts from friends and family.

There's no sign of any life, spirit or otherwise.

Mum rustles through the notes hanging off the bed, then doubles back to find the doctor to discuss Scarlett's progress. So I flop down in the brown flannel armchair by the window, pull it up close and start telling the story of my evening so far.

'Jack and I went back to the chapel,' I start excitedly, catching Scarlett's eyeballs writhe beneath her eyelids. 'You'll never guess what happened next...'

She doesn't reply though; she probably doesn't even hear me. But I've got used to people ignoring me recently. It's not just Scarlett, or Mum. It's everybody. Since her accident, nobody knows what to say to me, even Jack. I see it in their eyes.

Scarlett was always the outgoing one, the popular one. While she was out partying, I was at home studying. Yet she'd always do just as well as me at school, even better sometimes. It used to make me so angry at the time. But right now, it just makes me feel guilty that I ever thought that way.

There's nothing I wouldn't do to see her eyes open again. That's the thing about being a twin; you're only ever one half of something. It's not just going to university next year. There are so many things I can't imagine doing without Scarlett by my side.

I continue telling my story and I just get to the bit about the candles and the bracelet when the heart-rate monitor starts to race again.

For a split second I think that she's waking up.

But she's not.

That's when I realise… The bracelet!

Someone's going to have to go back and get it.

– Racing Daylight –

The bell tolls and the formal blazers of Saint Francis swirl in waves, smothering the more casually dressed sixth-formers in a sea of green. Hundreds of children run with excitement, whilst a few long-faced teachers patrol the edges, having long since forgotten what it feels like to be free.

'Jack, Jack, wait!' I shout, picking his biker jacket and spiked hair out of the heaving crowd. 'Jack, I just need to talk to you, it won't take long.'

I feel a sharp tug as he dives around the corner of the bike sheds, dragging me along by the sleeve.

'It's because of what happened at the chapel, isn't it?' he says, a large vein curling the width of his neck.

'Don't get riled up with me, Jack O'Connor, it was you who left me behind if you remember.'

'I didn't leave you. Let's just get that bit straight. I went to get help.'

'Really? Because that's not how it seemed to me.'

'Well, right now I don't care how it seems to you, I don't want to talk to you.' He holds a hand up to my face. 'What I really want is not to even see you!'

'I don't believe this. After all, it was your idea. You were the one who dragged me to that chapel after dark, and the moment it gets a little bit scary, you don't want to know.'

'It's not like that,' he says, pulling out a set of keys and a battered orange helmet from his bag. 'It's just

20

with all that's happening right now, I can't be dealing with ghosts as well.'

'But Jack, we've got to go back.' I raise my voice to compete with the whirling of his motor scooter. 'The bracelet, we've got to get the bracelet.'

'I can't hear you,' he says, burying his head into his helmet and revving the engine.

'Jack, wait up!' I shout, as he starts to pull away. 'I can't do it without you!'

I take a stroll across the new part of town, trying to summon the courage to swing by the chapel before it gets dark. The sun slouches in the sky, bouncing off the steel and glass structures of the new shopping centre on Auction Rise.

The centre only opened in the summer and it was probably the most exciting thing that happened to Burnham in over a hundred years. I remember when we were kids it used to be a live cattle-market – it was gross. Farmers would unload lorries full of animals in the street and then auction them off to the abattoirs. But now, with a multiplex cinema and big-brand department stores, it seems like a different world.

The haunted streets of the old town also seem worlds away too and my eyes happily wander amongst the lively shoppers and end-of-season sale signs. Eventually they linger on a long sparkling dress, wrapped around a mannequin in the window of River Island. It has matching shoes embroidered with hundreds of shiny stones, and a small clutch to boot.

The dress triggers a memory of Scarlett. She pointed it out to me on the day of her accident, saying she was going to buy it for the sixth-form ball.

I line up my reflection and try to imagine what it would look like on, holding my hair up in a bun and sucking in my sides so they no longer look like chubby fingers wrapped around a hotdog.

Still, it would never look right on me.

Scarlett, on the other hand, she'd look a million dollars in it. She was always the pretty one. Whereas I was the jealous one, somewhere in her shadow. She was even born ten minutes before me. I wasn't even planned: an accident, little more than the afterbirth really. Still, I'd happily buy that dress for her right now from my own pocket, if she'd only wake up.

The church bells chime five the moment I arrive at the central square, letting me know the hour of the day and what little light remains. The last breath of the Tuesday market hangs in the air. A few sorry traders are left clinging to the streets, their hands stuffed in their pockets like sparrows fluffing out their feathers on a winter's day, stubbornly trying to sell off the last of their goods so they don't have to load them back into their vans.

'Half a pound, a pound of bananas,' one crows, in a rhythm that vaguely resembles the chiming of the church bells.

'Plums, plums, get a handful of juicy ripe plums,' another cries.

Scarlett and I used to laugh about them when we were younger. We could never quite hear what they were saying in their own unique 'arable' brand of English. We always thought they were shouting out swear words in the centre of the street and then we'd copy them around the dinner table, much to Mum's delight!

Their voices echo into the distance as I slip under the portcullis of the Norman Tower. There's a loud clanging noise – my feet pounding the metal drawbridge and running on into the abbey. Giant fingers of jagged flint-stone stretch towards the sky, occasionally meeting in the odd archway, but on the whole sitting alone and abandoned. A few workmen are busy around them, preening the winter pansies and raking the perfectly manicured lawns.

I keep my head down, trying to avoid any attention, skipping across the grass in a desperate bid to save daylight. I hear a whistle from behind, but I carry on regardless, my eyes fixed on the cathedral up ahead. Its buffed sandstone glows against the amber sunset, gleaming like the centre of an ancient civilisation made entirely of gold.

A narrow path runs down the side, squeezing between its towering walls and a moat that circles the entire estate. I count two tiers of sixteen stained glass windows, filled with every colour you can imagine, each with its own story to tell. But right now I don't have time to hear them; I press on through to an orchard at the back.

A carpet of rusty-coloured leaves rustle beneath my feet; then my footsteps boom across the wooden footbridge that spans the Bream. Just beyond it, I pick up the same winding path that Jack and I followed last night, which cuts through the graveyard.

A low-lying mist clings to the undulating hills like a stretch-fit top, the lichen-clad tombstones poking their heads just above it, slouching towards the chapel in the distance.

I hurry through a rotten wooden gate, almost knocking it clean off its hinges, and work my way to the entrance around the rear. That's the thing about Burnham All-Saints Chapel. It's built back to front, facing to the west. That's why there are so many stories about it.

Most people in Burnham say it was a place of pagan worship, dating back before the abbey. Others even go so far to say devil worship, claiming it hides the gateway to hell. But everyone agrees, that it's the last place on Earth you'd want to be standing on your own in the dark.

The mist is sucked away by the lake opposite the entrance, unveiling a mysterious figure heading out of the chapel door. My heart thunders, wondering whether it's another ghost, before I recognise the gold and purple embroidery laced around his long white smock.

It's old Father Parfitt: part-time preacher, part-time teacher and full-time custodian of the abbey estate. He teaches me history, along with taking the odd assembly and giving talks on the abbey. The kids call him old Father Pervert, but there's no truth to it. He's just really old and unfortunately named, that's all.

'Father, just a moment,' I shout. 'I was hoping you might have found a bracelet that I dropped in the chapel, on, erm, Sunday?'

Luckily, old Parfitt doesn't hear me and continues on towards the rectory.

We both know I didn't have any business to be in the chapel on Sunday. As far as I know, it's not a working church for services. Not that I'm an expert or anything. It's been more than a while since my last confession. Mum just faked some Catholic aunt on Dad's side of the family to get us in at Saint Francis, because the grades there are better than Burnham Upper on the other side of town.

I rest my weight against the chapel door to get my breath back. Then I raise the strength to twist the rusted handle.

'Damn it! Old Parfitt must have locked it!'

With my hopes dashed, I sit awhile on the shingle pathway and stare across the dusky sky above the lake. I pick up a palm full of stones and start skimming them – bombarding an old mausoleum that sits alone on a little island. It's one of the few things I can remember

Dad teaching us when we were younger and I guess it's like riding a bike: something that you never forget.

From what I can recall Dad was a real outdoors type because the few memories that I do have of him all seem to involve either camping or fishing. But then again, he must have been a real free-spirited type too, because he popped out for a pint of milk one night and never came back.

That's how Mum tells the story anyway, but I'm old enough now to know there was more to it than that. But whatever type he was, he hasn't been much of a father. I'm sure he knows nothing about Scarlett's accident and I doubt he'd even care.

A milky sunset curdles in the mist as the remaining light gets lost behind the old mausoleum. The church bells chime half past five and it'll be pitch-black by six. So I admit defeat and start wandering back up towards the tower. I'm almost around the corner when I hear a loud creaking over my left shoulder.

Bolting around I see the chapel door slightly ajar. The few remaining skimming stones fall through my fingers, scattering to the ground. My chest tightens, my gut loosens, but for some reason that I can't explain, my feet betray my better judgement and lead me back down the path.

– For the Love of Our Sisters –

The last of the day races in ahead of me as I burst through the heavy wooden door. I search behind its shadow, surprised to see nobody there, before pulling the door to and stepping deeper inside.

Warmed by the last dregs of dusk, the old place barely looks any more inviting than it did last night. The smell of frankincense and damp compete in each nostril; a brass incense burner sits on the altar, chugging thin snakes of smoke into the air. My eyes quickly work their way down all six rows of red oak pews, like I'm skim-reading a long boring passage of text. Then I see Scarlett's bracelet, hanging off a cross carved into the armrest of the front row.

Running down the aisle I make a grab for it. But the back of a girl's head bolts up against the backrest. A gaunt withered hand reaches out, snatching the bracelet before I can get there.

'Hey! Give that back,' I shout, my voice drowned out by the sound of the girl crying.

I hesitate for a moment, unsure of what to do. Torn between sympathy and fear, I take a seat beside her. The girl's head falls back between her knees, but judging by her slim build and scruffy clothes, I'd say it's the same girl from last night, the one with the bright red eyes.

'Please, I just want the bracelet and I'll be gone,' I say.

'I saved it from the preacher man for you,' the girl replies, holding it out in her open hand, her head still buried between her knees. 'But he took the rest of your stuff and then he performed some sort of ritual.'

'I don't care about the other stuff, I just want that bracelet,' I say, trying to shut out her state of distress and the feeling that it stirs. 'It's my sister's and I've got to get it back to her as soon as possible.'

'Your sister's?' She places the bracelet in my open palm.

I cup my hand around the cold metal chain, clasping it tightly, and even though I'm free to leave, for some reason I don't. Instead I put my arm around the girl as she continues to sob.

'Come on, it's alright,' I say, trying to sound soothing.

'So how come your sister didn't come and get it for herself?'

'She's…' I pause, searching for the right word. 'Not well.'

'Not well? What's the matter with her?'

The girl pulls away from me, allowing me to get a good look at her face. Despite the state of her, she's a pretty little thing, pale-skinned, but with copper-coloured locks of curly hair and eyes that are no longer glowing red – they're as green as summer grass.

I hesitate a moment, lost in her pretty eyes. Suddenly I realise how strange it feels to be talking so openly with a ghost.

28

'My sister is sleeping,' I say.

'My sisters are sleeping too.'

Our eyes lock. A smile peeps through her tears, like a ray of sunshine through the clouds. We sit awhile without a word and a warm friendly silence stretches between us.

'I'm Rose,' I say, filling the emptiness and holding out my hand.

'Emily,' she replies, taking up my offer and dragging me to my feet.

She walks me up the aisle as if she's seeing me out, sending a strange tingling shooting up my back. Then all of a sudden she stops where Jack and I were sitting last night. I try to break away, but her grasp is too tight. For someone so thin, she seems remarkably strong.

'These are my sisters,' she says, holding her right hand above her head.

My eyes follow her flowing gesture, spotting several stone cherubs sitting amongst the wooden roof trusses: the ones I'd noticed last night.

'There were six of them yesterday,' I say.

'Yes, until you woke one up.'

Emily loosens her grip on my arm, but with my head still bent back and my neck arched everything becomes blurred. Thoughts swirl in circles through my mind; Emily's hands reaching out to me, and her bright red eyes, suddenly everything that happened last night makes perfect sense.

'Now I'm stuck here for eternity, unless I can wake up the others…' she says.

She continues to speak, but her words seem more distant. A multitude of feelings flow through my veins. Then my legs go weak and everything goes black.

I wake with my head resting on a musty hassock, wedged between Emily's knees. Her pretty face is the wrong way around and thick copper strands of hair tickle the end of my nose.

'It's alright,' she says, helping me to sit up and then squatting down in front of me. 'I think you fainted.'

'Really?' I'm still a little dazed. 'The last thing I remember was you telling me about your sisters and then…'

'Don't worry. I'll tell you another time. I think you were trying to leave. You said that you needed to get the bracelet back to *your* sister as soon as possible.'

'It's been a couple of weeks now. I don't suppose Scarlett is going to wake up in the next few minutes,' I say. 'And I'd like to hear about your sisters.'

'Well, there are the twins Evelyn and Madelyn.' She points up at two figures clutching at their midriffs. 'Then there's Alice the oldest, Hope the youngest and Paige in the middle.'

'So when did you all live here? When did you…'

'Die?' Emily pretends to choke herself and then laughs wildly. 'We lived here until the spring of 1692. That's when it happened. Can you believe it, six sisters all murdered in less than a week?'

'Murdered?' I say. 'How?'

Emily pauses awhile, unable to answer my question, or unwilling.

'Who would do such a thing?' I take her hands in mine. 'Why?'

'We were killed for our beliefs,' she says. 'We were the Sisters of Burnham All-Saints Chapel.'

'Oh, you were that kind of sisters,' I say, remembering from my history classes about troubles in the Church around those times. 'I thought you meant real sisters, like me and Scarlett.'

Emily throws my hands away from hers and frowns. 'We were real sisters. Closer than any family. I still feel their loss, their pain, the way they were taken from me.'

'You're right, I'm sorry,' I say. 'But didn't you say you can bring them back? Isn't that what you were saying just before I fainted?'

'Did I? No, I meant put them to rest. There's a book telling our story in the Clock Tower Museum in the centre of town. It's a special book. I need to bring it back here to the chapel where it belongs, so we can all rest in peace together. Tell me you'll help me get it back, please.'

'I don't know. I've got enough on mind with my sister Scarlett in a coma, my mum on the verge of a nervous breakdown and…'

'Come on,' she says, begging me with those pretty green eyes of hers. 'Once I lay them to rest I will return to the other side myself. Maybe I'll be able to find your

31

sister Scarlett trapped somewhere in-between. I'll bring her back to you, I promise.'

'Is that possible?'

'I'm almost sure of it.'

'I'm so desperate, I'll try anything.' I rummage through my bag for my phone. 'But right now, I've got to get home and visit the hospital with my mum.' I try to switch on my phone but the blasted battery is shot. 'Oh my god, what time is it?'

'I'm so sorry. It's my fault, isn't it? But you'll come back afterwards, won't you?'

'They lock up at seven,' I say in a panic, fastening Scarlett's bracelet around my wrist. 'I've got to go.'

'Meet me outside the abbey gate, just after the church bells chime twelve,' Emily says as I hurry down the aisle. 'Say you will, please…'

'I don't know,' I say, pulling the door open. 'I'm not promising anything.'

– Locking Up and Turning Out the Lights –

Moonlight streaks through the clouds, illuminating the shingle path that heads up to the gate. A flock of birds sweeps across the sky as I hurry through the graveyard. I try not to let my eyes follow – fixing them on the rickety footbridge that spans the Bream and leads onto the cathedral orchards. I must be halfway across it before I allow myself a look back at the chapel, poking its head through the mist like a priest on a parapet.

I narrow my eyes, squinting at the rusted clock face that fronts the tower, wondering if its hands still turn. Then something snatches my gaze from below. A hand fumbles its way over the top of one of the tombstones, followed by a head.

As the mist churns around the low-lying mounds of the graveyard, the dead rise, like lost souls of a shipwreck bobbing above the sea. At first limbs, then faces tearing through the fog and heading my way. I stall for a moment, my feet nailed to the wooden slats of the footbridge. Then my heart stabs the back of my throat as I feel a hand on my shoulder.

I turn to see a young man. He's wearing tight grey britches tucked into woollen socks and an old-fashioned flat-cap. He looks familiar; he's the market trader I saw from the car last night.

'I was wondering if I might see you again,' he says, flashing me a warm, lopsided grin. 'But this is no place for such a fine-looking lady to be walking unescorted.'

33

'I was just leaving.' I feel my face flush with embarrassment as he offers me his hand.

Despite his appalling dress sense, he's not bad looking and a damn sight more polite than the boys at Saint Francis. The church bells chime seven, startling me into life.

'Sorry, I've got to go,' I say, leaving him standing there with his hand still hanging.

'Well, you be careful roaming around here alone at night!' he shouts. 'There's dark goings on inside this abbey you know.'

My breath runs away from me as I sweep between the wind-clipped trees of the orchard. I crest a gentle rise and the mist slowly recedes, allowing the bright lights of the cathedral to brim over the horizon. I slow amongst the last staked saplings, spotting something unusual ahead.

Dozens of monks mill around the cathedral gardens, their bodies cloaked in long dark robes and their faces sheathed beneath their hoods. They're erecting a large wooden cross, pulling at guide ropes and hammering them to the floor, whilst a figure in white stands in the middle. He holds a flaming torch and wears a tall pointed hat, from which a few wisps of silver hair escape at the sides. From a distance he has a look of old Parfitt about him.

Once the cross is fixed into place, the monks take turns to lay wooden sticks at its base. Then they circle around the edges, lighting each other's torches and chanting in some ancient language.

Two more monks appear from the vestry, leading a young girl towards the centre. She's barely in her teens, slight and scruffy, with tangled hair that looks like it's never been washed. She gets lost for a moment amongst a sea of bodies.

Then I hear a scream.

The chanting gets louder before the circle breaks into two flanks and everything goes silent. I see the girl bound to the cross, her dress torn, baring her pale flesh for them all to see. The man in white slowly walks towards her and grips her firmly around the throat. Frantically she struggles, freeing one of her hands and scratching him across the face.

'Leave her alone!' I shout.

Then I lose my nerve and turn back towards the trees.

I break into a canter, weaving through the woods, the sound of footprints rustling behind. Dropping on all fours, I creep beside the iron railings that hug the riverbank, watching as the torches dance between the trees.

The hissing of the Bream covers my tracks. The moss-covered ground, littered with sharp flint-stones, bites at my hands and knees. It gives me an idea. Unearthing the largest rock I can find, I throw it deep into the brush behind me, sending them off my trail.

Then I sprint out of the cover of the trees and into the abbey ruins.

I snake between the tall flint-stone columns until I arrive at the centre. Silt-covered walls lie mostly unbroken in the footprint of a building. Several slim chambers sit beside a long narrow corridor that must be almost the height of my waist. I know it won't be long until the chasing monks catch up with me, so I drop back down to the ground and start crawling.

Up ahead there's a wide space that used to be the old cloisters, and beyond that the undamaged façade of the boarding house. Slit-thin windows circle around a grand archway and on the other side there's a path leading back up to the abbey gate.

I take a deep breath, focusing my thoughts on the opening. Then I jump to my feet and run.

'There she is!' A voice comes from over my shoulder.

Hooded figures swarm between the ruins and fill the void. I duck beneath an arm as one of the monks tries to grab me. I change my tack and two more figures collide into each other. Their thick squat frames are fat and slow, and just for a moment I think I'm going to make it.

Then I feel an arm tighten around my neck from behind and smother me. The musty smell of the man's cloak is suffocating. His sleeve flaps around my face. I sink my teeth into his fingers, scrape my foot down his shin, but still he won't let go.

Reaching backwards, I grab a handful of his unmentionables and give them a sharp twist. With that his grip finally loosens and I wrench myself free.

I sprint through the archway. The abbey gate looms ahead, voices chase from behind. My eyes are fixed on the steel portcullis, somehow still drawn. Then the mechanical grinding of jarring cogs fills the air and the sharp angry teeth start to lower to the ground.

'Hey, wait!' I shout upwards, to whoever is operating the pulley in the gantry.

But I don't think they hear.

The voices behind become more distant. The lowering gate gets closer and the grinding louder. I make it across the drawbridge and into the Norman Tower. Dropping to the ground, I roll, grazing my arms and legs on the uneven flagstones.

As I stare up, the sharp spikes close in on me. A breeze nibbles at my cheek as cold steel flashes past my face. Then there's a loud booming echo and the spikes fall flush into their fixings.

I struggle to my feet and a shiver runs up my back, as if someone danced across my grave. Grasping the crosshatched gate like a prisoner locked up in jail, I look back at the ruins. There's not a chasing monk in sight, but somehow I get the feeling that whoever was up there operating that pulley system didn't want me to escape.

My head is awash with unanswered questions. I wonder why the ghosts seemed to rise after dark and whether it's got something to do with Emily. I wonder about the girl I saw on the cross and whether she was lucky enough to escape too.

Realising that it's best not to wait around to find out, I turn around to make my way across town towards the hospital. I'm not surprised to see the Tuesday afternoon market has packed up and gone away, but I am shocked to see that once again, the little square is crawling with the dead.

Horse-drawn carriages clatter along the highway, whilst the heckling of money changing hands rings out across the street. I push my way through the busy crowds. The queues are so deep it's impossible to see what the stalls are selling, but the air is thick with the smell of fresh fish and cooked meat.

An old woman walks towards me. She's dressed in a long black shawl, her eyes are still, and her hands are fumbling out in front of her. 'Please, my girl,' she says, grabbing me by the sleeve. 'Please…'

'I don't suppose it's any use to you.' I pull out a couple of coins from my pocket. 'But here, take it.'

'No,' she replies sternly. 'Get going, my girl. You don't belong here. You don't belong amongst the dead. Be gone before they take you.'

Her grip tightens on my sleeve, her face creasing with worry.

'There she is!' I hear, shouted from behind.

Suddenly we're surrounded by monks. Three of them throw back their hoods and close in around us.

38

My heart beats wildly as I realise there's nowhere to run.

They get closer, their thick hairy forearms reaching out towards us. The blind woman clings to my arm, trying to hide behind me.

But much to my surprise, they grab her first, prising her fingers from my sleeve. She struggles, waving her arms wildly, sending them all into a tangled heap on the floor.

'Run, my girl!' she shouts. 'Run!'

I do as she says and head off into the crowd of people. Ducking and weaving, it's not hard to get lost, but somehow the image of her face remains burnt into the back of my eyes.

How the hell could she tell that I didn't belong here and what did they want with her?

Eventually I arrive at Suffolk General, where I'm met by the familiar sight of a man smoking in the doorway. He still has the intravenous drip in his arm and still has no shoes on. I guess he did make it to the morning after all.

The waiting room is emptier than ever. It's so quiet I can hear the ticking of the silver clock high up on the wall. It reads seven fifty-five, leaving me five minutes to head off Mum before the end of visiting hours.

I run through the twisting corridors and past the reception desk on Scarlett's ward, wondering what I'm going to use as an excuse for being late. Then suddenly I hear raised voices. Turning the corner, I see Mum

39

slumped in the brown flannel armchair beside Scarlett's bed and a crowd of hospital staff around her.

Barging my way through, I place an arm around Mum's shoulder as the doctor continues to speak. 'It's been over two weeks now, Mrs Glover. The swelling has come down and we can finally see what we are looking at.'

'And what are we looking at, Doctor?' Mum says angrily. 'Because to me it doesn't look as if anything is changing.'

'Well, the truth is that Scarlett is just not responding,' the doctor says. 'There's nothing in the way of brain activity, Mrs Glover. There hasn't been any for well over a week now.'

'And...?' Mum says.

The doctor looks down towards his notes as if he can't quite look my mother in the eye. 'Well, nothing is conclusive, but if she doesn't respond soon, then we may have to accept that there is nothing that we can do.'

'So what are you suggesting? Should we just turn the lights out, is that it?' Mum wails loudly. 'Save the electricity, so you can have the bed back?'

The doctor doesn't react, still not lifting his head from his notes.

'Get out!' Mum shouts. 'All of you! She'll wake up, she will, I know she will!'

'Okay, Mrs Glover, it's a lot to take in. I'll leave you alone with your daughter.' The doctor rustles his papers together and starts escorting the nurses away. 'We won't make any firm decisions about the future just yet.'

I don't know how long Mum and I sit there, staring silently at Scarlett. Sickness hangs heavy in the air as the ventilator rises up and down, and the monitor beside the bed beeps away steadily. Scarlett doesn't look any different than she did last night – still sleeping, still peaceful. All I know is that the stakes have been raised – things looked like they couldn't get any worse and now they have.

– The One-Eyed Monk –

I wait until Mum's asleep and all is quiet before creeping down the stairs and out the kitchen door. Gravel crunches underfoot as I hurry down the garden path, sneaking out of the back-gate and into the rat-runs that bend and twist behind Burnham's Victorian terraces. The thick stench of urine stains the air and algae ravages the drunken wooden fences that sway along Saint Mary's Walks.

The church bells chime midnight just as I burst out onto the main road, and a moment later, the streetlights go out. I run the red lights at the crossing to find the central square all but empty. The only sign of life is a single light left on at the Angel Hotel – although it's little comfort to the building itself. Creeping ivy scales its walls, sucking at the cement between its bricks, whilst its white-wooden window boxes lie empty for the winter.

Then I notice a girl standing alone in the shadows, her emerald eyes glistening beneath a dark blue headscarf.

'I was just about to give up on you,' Emily says, smiling.

'I've got to be honest, I nearly didn't make it,' I say. 'Things have got more serious with my sister, that's the only reason I came.'

'Oh, I'm so sorry.' Emily wraps her arms around me tightly. 'Is there anything they can do?'

'I'm not sure,' I say, my eyes welling with tears. 'The doctor wasn't clear, but he sounded really serious.'

Emily grazes her hands down my back and I lose myself in her pretty eyes for a moment. 'I promise you, that if you help me put my sisters to rest, then I'll help wake up yours,' she says.

'So what exactly do you need me to do?' I ask. 'You said something about the Clock Tower Museum.'

'That's right. That's where they're keeping the book I was telling you about – the book about my sisters.'

'So what do you need me for? The museum is just at the top of Angel Hill. Why don't you just go up there and grab it?'

'And how do you suppose I get inside?'

'Well, you're the ghost. Why don't you slip through the walls or something?'

'It doesn't quite work like that,' Emily laughs. 'I can't pass through walls any easier than you can. Well, not the ones that were standing when I was alive anyway.'

'So how did you get out of the abbey after they locked up, then?'

'I shimmied over the wall,' she replies, lifting her scruffy dress to show me her grazed shins.

'And the monks,' I say. 'Didn't they try to stop you?'

'Can you see them too?' Emily's eyes widen with excitement.

'It seems I can see all of the dead. The moment it got dark they all rose from their graves.'

'You must have really disturbed something,' Emily says. 'Either that or you've been cursed. I've never known someone living be able to see all of the dead before.'

'Can you fix it? Once we get you back to the other side, I mean.'

'I don't know. I guess so.'

'And those monks. What's the story with them?'

Emily grabs the top of my arms and starts to shake me. 'Now listen here, Rose,' she says sharply. 'Most of the dead are completely harmless. They're just going about their unfinished business, trying to put things right so they can put their souls to rest. But stay away from those monks. There's something not right about them, something strange and evil.'

'You're telling me. I caught them torturing a girl at the back of the cathedral. Then they dragged a blind woman away, right in front of me, only a few yards from here.'

'Lucky for me that Billy showed up when he did, otherwise they'd have grabbed me too,' Emily says.

'Who's Billy?'

'He's one of the market traders. He said he'd be coming back before the night is done and he reckons he knows someone who can get us into the Clock Tower.'

'So you met someone, who knows someone, who might be able to help,' I say. 'That sounds *really* promising, Emily. What makes you think he will do us any favours anyway?'

'You haven't met Billy,' Emily smiles. 'Let's just say he's got a bit of a weakness for the ladies.'

We wait for what seems like an eternity, until every spirit has left the little square and the last light has gone out at the Angel Hotel. Clouds thicken in the sky, smudging out the moon and making the night darker than before. The wind picks up too, gently blowing the street clear of leaves and leaving a chill in their place.

'Are you sure he's coming?' I say. 'I've got school in the morning.'

'Of course he's coming,' Emily says, as an old wooden milk wagon comes rolling in over the Humping Monks. 'In fact, I'm ready to bet that's him now.'

The driver pulls hard on the reins, dragging the little horse to a halt. Then a man leaps hurriedly off the back; he's wearing badly fitted britches pulled up to his armpits and he has a warm familiar smile.

'Billy Tanner at your service, ladies,' he says, tipping his cap and then whistling to the driver to pull away.

'It's a pleasure to meet you, Billy,' I say, holding out my hand.

'You're such a terrible liar,' Billy replies, playfully taking my fingers and turning my palm towards the ground.

'Why do you say that?'

45

'Firstly, we already met in the graveyard earlier.' He pushes his lips against the back of my hand. 'And secondly, although I never got your name, the pleasure is all mine.'

'Rose,' I say, feeling the blood rush to my face.

'Just like the colour of your cheeks,' Billy says.

'Jesus Christ! Do you two want me to get you a room at the Angel?' Emily says, striking me in the ribs with one of her sharp, bony elbows. 'It's just we've got a man to see about getting inside that museum.'

'Oh, do I sense a little jealousy there, my green-eyed lovely? Don't you worry, there's enough of Billy for the both of you.'

'I thought you were going to help,' Emily says, bringing him to order with those spellbinding eyes of hers. 'And just for the record, I wasn't worried and I certainly wasn't jealous.'

'Of course not,' Billy laughs. 'And of course I'm going to help. But first I'd like to show you ladies the night of your lives. If you're really lucky, I might even take you down to see the One-Eyed Monk.'

'You'll do nothing of the sort, you filthy beggar,' Emily protests.

'The One-Eyed Monk is a tavern.' Billy says, beaming. 'It serves the finest pint of Bishop's Finger this side of the Bream.'

'I knew what you meant,' Emily scowls, whilst Billy and I continue to snigger.

'It's not the most savoury place I've ever been, I'll grant you that,' Billy says. 'To tell you the truth, it's full of nothing but no goods and villains. But I got chatting to a fella over a few pints the other night. He goes by the name of *Pickawindow* Pete. Now don't get me wrong, he's a wrong 'un, but the right kind of wrong 'un, if you know what I mean. Says he used to be a locksmith, until he found out there was more money in breaking into places. He told me that there isn't a lock in the whole of Burnham that he can't open. He owes me a favour too.'

'So, what are we waiting for?' Emily steps between Billy and me and drags us both by the arms. 'For you two to get married and have babies?'

We hurry out of the main square and up Angel Hill. The windy lanes of Burnham's old town are lined with bow-walled, timber-framed buildings. Most of them are independent shops, selling overpriced tat to tourist.

Halfway up the slope, Billy breaks off ahead and beckons us down an alleyway to our right. I've never noticed it before; it's so narrow that with my arms outstretched I can touch both sides. It doesn't feel like it would lead anywhere pleasant. The uneven ground is littered with broken bottles, and flooded where rainwater has overflowed from the guttering.

'Mind your step,' Billy says, clambering over a large lifeless body wedged between the walls.

I look down at the sleeping man, his fat face folded where it's pushed against the brickwork and his open mouth slowly filling with water.

'Shouldn't we do something?' I say, turning to Emily. 'He might...'

'Die?' Emily laughs, shoving her arm into my back to hurry me. 'You've got a lot to learn about the dead.'

'What do you mean?'

'Well, how can someone die if they're already dead?' She crouches down and claps her hands either side of the man's face, forcing water to spout out of his mouth. 'He'll be right as rain this time tomorrow.'

'Emily! I can't believe you just did that,' I say. 'I thought you were a sister of the church and everything.'

'If there's one thing I've learnt from life,' she says, 'and from death for that matter, it's that all men can go to hell. Sisters have got to look after themselves.'

'And each other!' I add, pulling her along by the sleeve.

Billy is waiting for us at the end of the alleyway. His hand is held aloft as if he's about to feed the five thousand, pointing towards a wooden sign swinging above a doorway.

'My lovely ladies, may I present the One-Eyed Monk,' he says.

'I'm not sure about this,' I say, looking up at the faded picture of a hooded monk, half his face hidden beneath the shadow of his hood. 'It looks a bit dodgy to me.'

'Come on,' Emily puts her arm around my shoulders. 'You said it yourself; sisters have got to look out for each other.'

'Okay,' I say. 'But let's find this Pete and get straight out of here. I don't like the look of this place one bit.'

'And nor should you.' Billy beckons us towards the door. 'Half of the scum in here would steal all your money and leave you bleeding in the alleyway, just for looking at them the wrong way.'

'And the other half?' I ask.

'Oh, they'd do exactly the same,' he grins. 'Only they'd have their wicked way with your twitching corpse afterwards.'

We stagger down three steps, stooping below a thick wooden roof truss. My eyes scan the badly lit room, sizing it up. It's a low-ceilinged building, filled to the rafters with rough-looking men who look like the front row of a rugby scrum. There's an open fire roaring away in the chimneystack to the right, blowing a thick blanket of smoke across the room. Exposed beams form dark alcoves in the other corner, where even darker-looking men sit on upturned barrels playing cards.

'So how the hell do we find Pete?' I shout, putting my mouth close to Billy's ear.

'Oh, we'll bump into him sooner or later, don't you worry about that. But in the meantime, try to blend in. Do what everyone else does.'

'Like what?' I ask.

49

'Drink!' shouts Billy, dragging us towards the bar, where the sound of badly played music blares in from a room at the back. 'I'll have three pints of your best Bishop's Finger, my good sir.'

The landlord nods without a word.

He's a tall man, his bony chest poking out of his unbuttoned shirt and his greasy hair swept back in a ponytail. He takes down three glass tankards from a shelf and lines them up below a brass lever. His dark brown eyes work me up and down as he heaves on the pump, filling the glasses with a rusty-coloured slop.

'Will that be all?' he asks.

'Well, we've got a couple of One-Eyed virgins here,' Billy smirks. 'So best we have three shots of tree-sap vodka to chase them down.'

The other men lined along the bar begin to chatter. I feel the weight of their eyes on my body, like a pack of hungry dogs staring at their dinner.

'Well, surely you can see that we've both got two eyes,' Emily says, fluttering her eyelashes at them. 'Oh and just for the record, we're not virgins either!'

Cries of laughter race along the bar and the landlord accidentally overflows the little wooden cups of vodka. The man next to me is so amused that he spits out his drink and sprays it all over me.

'I'm so sorry, how terribly rude of me,' he says, pulling out a handkerchief and dabbing it on my chest. He looks a little out of place here: well-spoken, and wearing a navy-blue jacket with polished brass buttons. 'I'm Roland, but my friends call me Roly.'

'It's absolutely fine, Roly,' I say, drawing his attention to his wandering hands. 'I'm sure we can be friends. But not *that* good friends, if you know what I mean?'

'Oops, I beg your pardon again. Well, let me at least offer you some advice if you're going to drink that stuff.'

'You're offering *me* advice on holding down *my* drink,' I say, smiling. 'It seems kind of odd considering I'm still wearing half of yours.'

'Point taken, but you don't get like this without learning a little bit along the way.' He points at his red potato nose and pokes out his stomach so that it bulges over the top of his trousers. 'You want to drink the vodka first, but be quick about it, and hold onto your nose too. Its bark is far worse than its bite. But it's still going to burn a little on the way down – that's why it's best to keep your beer at the ready.'

'Okay, hold my nose, down the vodka, and then wash it down with my beer. I think I've got all of that.'

'Half a crown she coughs it up,' a scrawny man interrupts, pushing his way in from behind.

'If it isn't my old friend *Fourfingers*,' Billy says, pretending to shake the man's hand before pulling away and making fun of the missing digit on his right hand. 'You should know better than making bets you can't cover.'

'I can cover this one,' Fourfingers replies. 'Besides, it'll give me a chance to get even with you from yesterday.'

'You're on,' Billy says, downing his shot with ease and then sipping at his beer casually. 'Ladies, hold onto your noses, along with your guts.'

I raise the little wooden cup to my pursed lips, my other hand clamped around my nostrils. Then I close my eyes and throw back my head. A scorching shaves the back of my throat, pulling my gums back over my teeth and burning all the way down my gullet.

I fumble for my pint, eyes still closed, dousing the fire with a large gulp and wiping my mouth with my sleeve. I turn to Emily who's already finished hers and is slamming the little wooden cup stiffly onto the bar.

There's a loud cheer. Roly slaps me hard on the back.

'Well done, ladies!' he says. 'It looks like we have a winner.'

Fourfingers empties his pockets to reveal nothing but the brown lining of his trousers and a few wisps of pipe tobacco.

'Cough up!' the landlord says. 'You know what happens to those that don't settle their debts in my house.'

'It's no bother,' Billy adds, a crowd swarming around them both. 'I don't mind letting it slide this once. For old times' sake.'

'It's not your place to let it slide,' the landlord says.

Two burly men grab Fourfingers and hold him face down against the bar. The landlord hands Billy a gold coin for his trouble, then pulls out a paper scroll and a large feather from a cupboard. 'I Silas Samuels, landlord of the One-Eyed Monk, do hereby lay rights to the soul of Francis Fourfingers, in settlement of his debts,' he says. 'Do you have any last requests?'

Fourfingers' hand is forced open, his palm quivering. 'No, no, I'll pay tomorrow, I'll pay,' he shouts, as the landlord pulls out a large curved blade from a scabbard on his belt.

Silas draws the blade across Fourfingers' hand and blood gushes out all over the bar. Then he stems the bleeding with the paper scroll, before pinning it to the wall with his knife. 'That should hold it for the time being,' he says. 'Now, how about a drink to seal the deal? On the house of course.'

Fourfingers huddles like a stray dog over his pint, clutching at his wounded hand. I stare at him for a moment as the mood along the bar slowly starts to settle. Then Billy grabs my arm and drags me away towards the fireplace.

'What the hell was all that about?' I ask.

'Well, there's only one rule at the One-Eyed Monk,' Billy says, sipping at his beer. 'You always pay your debts.'

'And what will happen to Fourfingers now?'
'By the time the blood dries on that paper, he'll be no more,' Billy replies. 'Like your friend said, you might

not be able to kill the dead, but a spirit can't walk the Earth without a soul.'

I take a look back across the room. Fourfingers is nowhere to be seen. There's just half a pint and an empty space at the bar in his place.

'And what does the landlord want with people's souls anyway?' I say.

'Well, rumour has it old Silas used to be a stagecoach robber, until he wound up winning this place in a game of cards,' Billy says. 'They say he's been here ever since, collecting souls, trying to buy his way in to heaven.'

'Can you do that?' I say, turning to Emily. 'Can you buy your way into heaven?'

'How should I know? But I guess with enough souls, anything is possible.'

'And how many is enough?'

'Now that depends what you've done.' Billy downs the last of his beer and wipes the froth from his lip.

'So what's your story, Billy?' I ask, changing the subject. 'Why are you here?'

'I don't know what you mean. I'm having a beer, showing you two ladies the night of your lives.'

'No, Emily says that all the dead are just going about their business. Trying to work out how to put their souls to rest.'

'Business?' Billy says. 'Me and my old man are going into the women's clothing business. I won a pitch on the market from Fourfingers in a game of brag. And tomorrow night my old man is arriving at the Dry Dock with a boat full of stock.'

'That's not what I meant,' I say. 'Is there something that you didn't get around to finishing before you died?'

At that moment the music stops playing from the room at the back. There are a couple of loud crashes, followed by a tense silence. Then the music starts up again, even more out of tune than it was before, and everyone carries on as if nothing happened.

'You two wait here.' Billy slams down his empty glass on the mantelpiece. 'I'll go and see what that was all about.'

'No, I'd rather come too,' I say. 'By the look of some of these men, I'd say it's been a long while since they last enjoyed the company of a woman.'

'Fair enough,' says Billy, taking both me and Emily by the arm. 'But stay close, it's a long way to the door if things get rough.'

We burst into the backroom. It's far from splendid, but a step up in class from the bar. Candlelit chandeliers swing from the ceiling and the walls are covered in fancy wallpaper with thin gold pinstripes. A four-piece band plays on a raised stage to our left, no longer protected by a row of balustrades, which now lay strewn across the floor.

Drunken men sway from side to side with little regard for the rhythm of the music, whilst half-naked ladies dance between them, money pouring out of their frilly bras and knickers.

Billy drags us through the trail of destruction towards a shattered window at the back. He puts his shoulder to the door beside it and we spill out into a courtyard.

A sobering gust of air wafts into my face. Then I spot a skinny man lying in a puddle of his own blood, while a larger man crouches over him, rifling through his pockets.

'Pete, what happened?' Billy shouts.

'I pray he means the one who's still conscious,' Emily says, whispering in my ear.

'Friend of yours?' the big man replies, not even having the decency to stop robbing his victim. 'I always thought his name was Pickawindow.'

'Friend? More of a business acquaintance really,' Billy replies, holding his hands up defensively. 'They call him Pickawindow because he used to be a locksmith.'

The large man lets out a booming belly laugh as he takes a ring of keys from around Pete's neck. 'That may be true, but that isn't why we call him Pickawindow. It's because his hands like to touch more than they can afford and someone always has to ask him to leave.'

'That someone being you?' Emily asks. 'Oh and let me guess, you let him choose which window he leaves from, too?'

'You're a smart one,' the man replies, slowly starting to rise. 'A pretty one too. I could find work for a girl like you.'

Standing up, he must be all of six foot five; his dark, curly hair is matted in tangles and disappears into an unkempt beard. 'Now that's a pretty thing as well,' he says, pawing at Scarlett's bracelet on my wrist. 'You don't see many like that around these parts.'

'Don't touch it!' I say, slapping his hand. 'It's not even mine.'

'Oh, feisty one!' the man says. 'Why don't you two come and work for Uncle Bran? I've got punters who'd go crazy for a double act like yours.'

'Come on, let's get out of here,' I say, turning to Emily.

'Not without those keys,' she says.

'Oh, you want these?' Bran waves Pete's ring of keys in front of her nose. 'I'm sure we can come to some sort of arrangement.'

'Half a crown?' Billy says bravely, offering him the gold coin he won at the bar.

Bran lets out another booming laugh.

'Half a crown for an old set of keys?' he says. 'They must be worth an awful lot to you, if you're willing to pay half a crown for them. How about you throw in that bracelet of hers and allow these two lovely ladies to spend the rest of the night working off the balance.'

'No chance,' Billy says calmly. 'But how about a friendly little wager – her bracelet against your set of keys?'

'If you're thinking about a drinking contest, you can forget it. I've seen your girls in action at the bar.'

'Cards?' Billy holds out his palm.

'Billy, it's not mine to lose!' I say.

But it's too late. Billy is already shaking Bran's hand.

– Double or Nothing –

We make our way back into a dimly lit corner of the bar room, where several upturned barrels are positioned around a huge hunk of rough-cut wood. Bran takes a seat first and starts emptying the contents of his pockets onto the table – three hand-rolled stogies, a giant box of cook's matches and a four-inch cigar whittler with a polished ivory handle.

'So let's get the rules straight, pretty boy,' he says, striking a match against the rough tabletop and lighting up a cigar. 'You put in your girl's bracelet and I'll put in the keys. We'll play three-card brag for a pot of matches and the winner takes the lot.'

'Sounds straight enough,' Billy says. 'So put the keys on the table and let's get started.'

'That's a good one,' Bran laughs, breaking open the matchbox and spilling its contents across the table. 'Stump up the bracelet first, unless you want me to take it still chained to your lady's wrist.'

'No, you first,' Billy says.

'Really, gentlemen.' Emily takes off her headscarf and steals their attention by shaking free her copper-coloured hair. 'Put them both in here and I'll hold on to them until we're done.'

'Are you alright with that?' Billy says, unclasping Scarlett's bracelet and handing it to Emily. 'I'll win it back for you. I promise.'

'Of course he will,' Bran says. 'And if he doesn't, I just might let you keep it; as long as you come and work for Uncle Bran for a couple of nights. I've got punters that would go crazy for a little warm flesh.'

'I won't let it come to that,' Emily says, dropping my bracelet into her headscarf. 'Now, the keys, Bran.'

'Alright, don't get your panties in a twist.' He throws her the ring of keys. 'But you run out on me before the game is done and I'll cut those pretty little eyes straight off your face, thread them through a lock of that lovely curly hair and make a bracelet of my own. Do you hear me?'

There's a strained silence as Emily stares at Bran. Their eyes lock together like two dogs sizing each other up in an alleyway, until a familiar voice cuts between them.

'Do I sense a game about to begin?'

It's old Roly, from the bar earlier. He's holding a silver serving tray, lined with five glass tankards of beer that are circled around a pack of sealed playing cards.

'Compliments of Silas, the landlord.' He places the tray down in the middle of the table. 'Do you mind me asking what you're playing for?'

'It's a private game for a rusty set of keys and a worthless bracelet,' Bran says. 'Nothing to get excited about.'

'Your bracelet?' Roly places his hand on my shoulder. 'I noticed it earlier. It's a fine-looking piece. I'd happily give you a couple of shillings for it.'

60

'No, it's not for sale,' I say. 'My friends and I just want that set of keys.'

'I tell you what,' Bran says, 'why don't you throw a couple of shillings into the pot and join us? If that's alright with Billy boy, of course.'

'Well, I'm not sure about that,' Roly replies. 'I'm not really a gambling man and the bracelet isn't worth much more than that to buy.'

'Why don't you shut up and let the real men get on with their game then,' Bran replies.

'Oh, go on then. I guess a little game of cards might be fun,' Roly says, tossing a handful of brass pennies into Emily's headscarf and sitting down. 'But you might have to teach me the rules.'

Bran breaks the seal on the cards and quickly thumbs through the pack before handing them on to Emily to deal. 'Three cards each and no shuffling. Can you manage that pretty eyes?'

Emily nods and starts handing out the cards one by one. From what I can gather the rules are much the same as poker, but with a few less cards.

Billy gets off to a good start with a pair of tens and goes in big straight away, throwing in six matches. Roly baulks at the first opportunity, leaving Billy head to head with Bran.

'Well, let's see what you're made of then, big man,' Billy says, raising the stakes even higher.

'Look at you, *Billy Big Potatoes*.' Bran narrows his eyes as he meets Billy's stake. 'You know, you're not the first pretty boy to come in here with a couple of ladies on his arm, thinking he knows how to play brag. But in my experience, the younger they are, the less they really have to brag about. So I'm going to pull your britches down in front of these pretty girls and show them exactly what you're working with.'

'Is that right?' Billy says, laying his cards onto the table with a smile. 'Because sitting here on this barrel, it seems that I'm staring down at a pair of tens.'

'But take a good look around, Billy boy,' Bran says, savouring a long pull on his cigar and puffing out a thick cloud into Billy's face. 'If you look really hard, you might just notice that in the end, all the ladies wind up in Uncle Bran's hands.'

Then he flashes three queens and uses them to scoop the pile of matches across the table.

'Billy!' I say, punching him on the arm. 'I thought you knew what you're doing.'

'Don't worry, I'm just warming up.' He hands me the gold coin he won from his bet with Fourfingers. 'Keep the drinks coming and I'll turn the game around before you're back.'

The beer keeps flowing, the matches move around the table in tides, and by the fourth round of drinks Billy and Bran are almost level. But it's Roly who's the surprise leader. He's been choosing to play blind, which means his cards remain face down but he only puts in half the stake. And somehow, it seems to be working.

I feel the drink going to my head and the room begins to spin a little. So I cling to Billy's arm, as much for balance as for comfort.

Emily continues dealing, Roly remains silent, whilst Bran and Billy carry on bickering like a couple of school children.

Billy gets dealt a bum hand, but bluffs it out for a while to see what the others are holding. Roly goes along with it, staying blind, of course. Then Bran suddenly ups the stakes, throwing in all of his pot at once and everyone falls silent.

'Bully boy tactics from the big man! Now that's a surprise,' Billy says, throwing his cards into the middle to fold. 'I guess this one is yours – unless the blind man wants to call your bluff?'

All eyes turn to Roly. He strokes his chin with his thumb and forefinger, pausing awhile before finally clearing his throat. 'I guess it's a small price to pay, to let a blind man see again,' he says, not even having to put in half of his pile to match Bran. 'You can count me in.'

'Well, you're not going to want to see this.' Bran fans his cards out across the table, grinning broadly. 'Queen, king, ace. I make that a royal flush.'

He reaches one of his giant hands towards the pot.

'Not too hasty, my old chum,' says Roly, slowly peeling his cards off the table one at a time, to reveal three sevens. 'I believe three of a kind beats a royal flush.'

Bran rises up off his stool, his teeth bared over his gums, but no longer smiling. 'I believe it does, old man, but I'm not buying it.'

'Well, that's lucky, because I'm not selling it.' Roly's voice quivers slightly. 'I'm playing cards for it. And by the look of things, I've just cleaned you out.'

'No, I'm not buying the fact that you appeared from nowhere with a sealed pack of cards, and all of a sudden, you've pulled three sevens out of your blind backside,' Bran says, grabbing Roly by the short hairs curling out the back of his head. 'In fact, I'm willing to bet these cards are marked.'

Billy jumps to his feet. 'Come on, Bran, you know what happens if you don't settle up.'

Suddenly the whole room seems to be watching us. The beer pumps stop flowing, cards stop being dealt and silence spreads across the room like a plague of Black Death.

Bran is first to breach the peace, driving Roly's head into the table and smashing it to a pulp. Billy wades in with a couple of punches that get soaked up by Bran's bulk. Then Bran slaps him with a backhander that catapults Billy halfway across the room.

Tables turn over, bottles go flying and a full-scale riot erupts. Bran sees his chance and reaches for Emily's headscarf. But before his grip can tighten around it, Emily steals his cigar cutter and stabs it through his hand.

His fingers writhe like live eels thrown into a bucket of boiling water. He stands there, nailed to the table, pain etched across his face. Then Emily snatches her headscarf off the table and with the weight of the keys and Roly's pennies still inside, she starts bludgeoning Bran around the head with it.

I scan the room for Billy, but he's nowhere to be seen. A glass comes whistling past my ear and smashes against the wall. My feet get swept away from me and I drop to the floor. Within a couple of seconds, I'm drowned in a sea of hobnail boots. My fingers get trodden on and my face is kicked, sending my front teeth straight through my lower lip.

Then a hand bursts through the crowd and pulls me to the surface. 'Come on,' Emily says. 'Let's get out of here.'

'But what about Billy?'

'Billy can take care of himself,' she says, dragging me out of the door by my sleeve.

Voices chase us down the alleyway. We leap over the lifeless man who's still wedged in the gap. I overtake Emily as we round the corner, blood trickling down my chin. We run past the little shops, our feet pounding the wet cobbled stones of Angel Hill.

Eventually I come to rest in the very centre of the old market square. Half a second later, Emily clatters into the back of me. We stand there for a moment, our hands locked together, holding each other up.

'Remind me never to get on the wrong side of you,' I say, my breath still coming in short gasps. 'Did you get my bracelet?'

'That's not all I got,' Emily says, dragging me over towards the Angel Hotel. We slump down on the steps overlooking the abbey gate and she opens up her headscarf. 'One bracelet for you, a rusty set of keys for me, a handful of pennies and...' She reaches a hand down into her cleavage. 'A bottle of tree-sap vodka that's still half full.'

'You're wild,' I say, snatching the vodka and taking a swig. 'But seriously, we should've waited for Billy.'

'Rose, Billy is dead,' Emily replies. 'But he died hundreds of years ago and they can't steal his soul. Either Roly was cheating or Bran didn't settle up his debts. Whatever happened, Billy didn't do anything wrong.'

'I guess you're right,' I say, offering her the bottle. 'But I still think we should have waited for him.'

'That's because you're sweet on him,' Emily says, laughing.

'I am not. But you have to admit, he did show us one hell of a night. Other than school and the endless trips back and forwards to the hospital, I've barely been anywhere since the accident. I think I needed a night out.'

'For our sisters!' Emily throws back the vodka and wipes her mouth on her sleeve. 'Although you never did tell me what happened to your sister Scarlett.'

'Didn't I?' I snatch the bottle back and take a large gulp. 'You must be the only person in Burnham that doesn't know what happened that night.'

'How did she end up in a coma?'

'It was our birthday, two weeks ago today,' I say, with a cold shiver shuddering up my spine. 'The nightlife around here in the midweek has got less *life* to it than the One-Eyed Monk. So me, Jack and Scarlett just went out for a meal. We were going to go out properly at the weekend.'

'And?' Emily says. 'How do you end up in a coma after a meal?'

'Well, Jack kept us entertained all night by telling us these ghost stories about the chapel. He says it's got something to do with devil worshippers, and that hidden beneath the floor is the gateway to hell.'

'My chapel?' Emily laughs. 'It might have the odd ghost, I'll grant you that. But devil worshipping? Don't be so ridiculous.'

'I don't know why we agreed,' I say. 'But on the way home Jack had this idea of breaking into the abbey and finishing off the last bottle of wine outside the chapel. He helped us onto the wall and he and I climbed down the other side, no problem. But Scarlett, being Scarlett, she had to show off. She tried to walk along the top in seven-inch heels.'

I pause for a moment, taking another large gulp of vodka that finds the cut on my lip and makes me wince.

'She didn't even fall that far,' I say. 'But she hit her head on something hard, solid flint-stone or something. Her eyes have never opened since.'

'So that's why you and Jack came back to the chapel last night,' Emily says. 'To see if her spirit was still there?'

'Something like that. Although it sounds stupid when you say it out loud.'

'Any more stupid than sharing a drink with a three-hundred-year-old ghost?' Emily grabs back the bottle. 'Anyway, I promise that from tomorrow night, we'll start putting my sisters to rest. And once we're done, we'll do what we can to wake yours up.'

'I'm not sure I can manage another night like this again.'

'Of course you can,' Emily grins, downing the last swig of vodka. 'Like you said, you don't want to get on the wrong side of me.'

– The Hangover From Hell –

A piercing noise splits through my head and wakes me with a start. I fumble through the covers and blindly strike out at my bedside table until it stops. My eyes peel open, but my tongue remains stuck to the roof of my mouth, which tastes like a spider has crawled inside and died during the night.

I stumble downstairs to find half a pot of coffee and two slices of charred toast on the kitchen table. Mum always leaves me breakfast, even though she has to leave well before I wake up. Despite Scarlett's accident, she continues to work two jobs. She says she has no choice if we want to keep a roof over our head.

By the time I'm out of bed, she's already done the cleaning at All-Saints Primary School and then she's off to the old people's home to work the day shift. And although I know she went to a lot of trouble to leave me something to eat, the very thought of it makes my stomach turn over, so I decide to give breakfast a miss and go back upstairs to make myself look presentable.

It takes me quite some time to wash away the stains of last night and by the time I arrive at the school gates, the second bell is already ringing for the end of registration. I stagger across the playground, my hair still wet and my head spinning with a raging hangover.

From the front Saint Francis looks like your typical Victorian school building. Its red brick walls a little off ninety, large sash windows spread over three floors, and

69

a tall bell tower dominating one side. But despite its humble façade, Mum says it's the best state school in the whole country. She says it's down to their *good old-fashioned* approach to discipline and you practically have to put your name down at birth to get in.

I follow the masses of green blazers through the corridors, my head down, trying to avoid any attention. The whitewashed walls are lined with endless rows of religious portraits: former bishops of Burnham Abbey and dead saints, mostly. Then there's a huge wooden plaque just before the entrance to the main hall. It bears the name of every head boy and girl, dating back to the beginning of the nineteen hundreds.

Somewhere at the bottom is Scarlett's name. I can still picture Mum's face when she found out. It made her so proud. I wasn't so impressed, but there you go. I just don't know how she did it. She spends most of her lessons talking over the teacher, she never studies at home and I'm not sure she even knows where the library is. But that's Scarlett for you. She has this way of always landing on her feet, whatever life throws at her.

That's why I know she's going to wake up.

Relief sets in as I make it to the glass atrium, which leads onto the purpose-built sixth-form centre at the back. I hate walking the school corridors at the moment. It feels as if everybody is watching me. I can almost hear what they're whispering as I pass.

That's her, the girl whose sister is in a coma.

70

I heard the whole family is cursed by the devil.

I wish Scarlett were here. She'd never stand for it!

Finally I arrive at the history block. Standing in the doorway is old Father Parfitt, his white clerical collar protruding above a crisply ironed black shirt.

'Year Thirteen, I should not have to remind you that today's lesson is under exam conditions,' he says loudly, causing silence to spread the entire length of the corridor.

One by one we pass him by, taking the bare essentials of a pen and ruler from our bags, before being directed to a seat. I'm at the very end of the line and when my time comes, I stop right in front of him, glaring up at his face.

I scan his wrinkled forehead, his eyes set behind dark grey circles, and his balding scalp shining through a few wayward wisps of silver hair. He stands his ground, his eyes holding mine tightly for a moment. Then I notice his jawline, freshly shaven, but without a single scratch in sight.

I guess it can't have been him that I saw in the abbey last night.

My gaze falls and fixes on a piece of jewellery tied around his neck. It's a three-inch metal crucifix on a dark leather strap. I imagine most priests wear something similar, but this figure of Christ isn't like anything I've ever seen before. Instead of lying back in acceptance, he's leaning forward, arms tensed, looking almost angry. There's something unnerving about it. So

71

I hurry past and take the last available seat in the front row.

'It is now exactly nine thirty,' Parfitt says, closing the door. 'Year Thirteen, you have until eleven fifteen. Please begin.'

I scribble my name on the cover page. Then, forcing open the seal at the top of the paper with my ruler, I read the first question.

Study the six sources of information about the Suffolk Witchcraft Trials of 1692 and then answer three of the six sub questions.

Suddenly things start to make sense: the monks inside the abbey, the girl on the cross being tortured, the blind lady being dragged away. That's what those dead monks were up to. They were conducting witchcraft trials.

I begin writing, jotting down the first random thoughts that come into my mind. But my head still bangs from last night. And to make matters worse, Parfitt insists on pacing around the room. His polished brogues strike the tiled floor, squeaking as he turns like a regimental soldier at the end of each row. The noise reverberates around my head, making it impossible to concentrate.

I don't get much more than a page down before Parfitt calls time and starts to collect in the papers. In fact by the time we're dismissed, I feel so drained that I decide to slope off home. To be fair, the rest of the day was only meant to be spent at the Records Office doing history coursework and I'm sure nobody will notice that I'm not there.

Mum and I visit Scarlett again in the evening, although Mum only spends a couple of minutes at her bedside before the doctor ushers her into his office.

They don't invite me in, which really annoys me. After all she's my sister and I'm eighteen, not a child. I've got a right to know what they're talking about.

'Scarlett,' I say, clinging to her lifeless hand beside her bed. 'Don't worry, I'm going to find a way to wake you up.'

The heart-rate monitor doesn't respond, but I swear I feel her grip tighten around my fingers.

'I won't let them turn you off,' I say. 'I've found someone who can help.'

I carry on talking, even though I know she's not listening. There's something therapeutic about it, sitting there unloading my worries. I tell her all about Emily and Billy and the One-Eyed Monk. It's not like I could tell anyone else – they'd probably think I'd gone mad.

It makes me realise that Scarlett and I never used to talk like this, even when she was awake.

Other than birthdays and special occasions, Scarlett was far too busy to spend time with me. And although it pains me to admit it, I found her a little bit superficial, bordering on self-obsessed.

Mum goes straight to bed when we get home and I pretend to do the same. But on the stroke of midnight, I sneak out the back gate and into Saint Mary's Walks.

Rain lashes down from the sky and my feet splash in deep puddles along the way.

Thankfully Emily is waiting outside the abbey when I arrive, although she looks like she's been stood there awhile. Her copper-coloured hair is plastered to her skin, and a damp leather satchel is slung across her shoulder.

'I'm surprised to see you again,' she says, wrapping her bony arms around me. 'I thought last night might have scared you off.'

'You shouldn't have worried. But promise me one thing. Promise me there's no vodka in your plan again tonight.'

Emily stares at me with those pretty green eyes of hers and smiles. 'I can't promise that. But I will try.'

She takes me by the arm and leads me up Angel Hill. As we crest the gentle rise, I see light searing through a glass clock-face, beaming out in all directions and stroking the wet pavement below. Like most of the buildings in the old town, the museum's walls are made from flint-stone reclaimed from the abbey. But there's something sinister about it: a tall crooked tower that stretches above all the other rooftops in the town, always lit, scraping away at the sky like a long black fingernail.

The closer we get, the faster my heart begins to beat.

74

'So you keep watch,' Emily says, as we huddle inside a wooden porch that surrounds the entrance. 'And I'll find out whether these keys were worth all the trouble that they caused us.'

The storm from earlier has blown over and the streets lie empty and still. The living residents of Burnham have long since retired for the night and the dead are mostly off their heads in the One-Eyed Monk. But then footsteps start to strike the cobbled paving stones. Quietly at first, with a slow measured rhythm, pounding through my head for the second time today.

'Emily, there's someone coming,' I say in a whisper.

A tall white hat peeps over the brow of Angel Hill. Emily pushes me hard against the side of the porch, covering my face with her arm and draping her sackcloth dress around my body.

'Don't make a sound,' she says. 'Don't even breathe.'

'That's easy for you,' I say, peeking out from under her sleeve, desperate to get a better look. 'You're already dead.'

A man approaches, a long white gown billowing behind him.

'It's him,' I say, unable to control my excitement any longer. 'The man I saw in the abbey last night.'

A beam of light from the clock tower catches him square on, caressing the contours of his face. The church bells strike one. Our eyes meet and time stands still for a moment. A bead of perspiration trickles down my back and I tighten my grip around Emily's waist

'It's Father Parfitt,' I say under my breath. 'I don't believe it!'

The man in white pauses a moment, no more than ten yards away from us. Then he lifts up his hat, scratches at his balding head like he's forgotten something, and turns back down the hill.

'Jesus!' Emily says. 'You look like you just saw a ghost.'

'Worse than that,' I say. 'I think I just saw my history teacher.'

'Well, luckily he didn't see us. I told you not to make a sound.'

'I know, but I'm pretty sure he's the same man I saw in the abbey last night. My history teacher, sacrificing witches with a group of dead monks.'

'Sacrificing witches?'

'Yes, it was on my exam paper today,' I say. 'That's what those monks were up to last night.'

'It wouldn't surprise me,' Emily says. 'Nothing would surprise me about *them*. Come on. Let's get inside, before he comes back with more.'

She forces the last rusty key into the lock and starts rattling it around. For a moment it seems as if it doesn't fit. Then there's a loud clunking noise and the latch turns over.

'I bet we're the first people to break in here in nearly a thousand years,' Emily says, grinning broadly. 'Probably the only people.'

'How can you be so sure?'

'You do know what this used to be?' she says, slowly pushing open the door. 'They did teach you about that in your history class, didn't they?'

I stare back at her blankly. 'Nope. I haven't been around this place since I was at primary school.'

'It was a prison.' Emily flashes me another smile. 'Now, are you coming in or what?'

I keep a hand on her shoulder as we step inside. Other than a few streaks of light piecing through the barred windows, we're in complete darkness. It takes a moment for my eyes to adjust. But pretty soon I can make out a cash register on the desk in front of us. Then there's a range of torture devices scattered around the room: old-fashioned wooden stocks, an iron rack and long chains manacled to the walls.

'So Emily, where's this book of yours?' I ask.

'Up there,' she says, pointing to a curved stone staircase on the far side of the room.

'So what are we waiting for? Let's go and grab it.'

'One of us needs to wait here. To keep watch for the monks.'

'I don't like the idea of being left here alone.'

'Well, you go and get the book, while I keep watch then,' Emily says.

'I don't like the idea of going up there on my own either.'

'Fine!' Emily says sharply. 'Stone, paper, scissors you for it. The loser goes to get the book and the winner keeps watch.'

'Okay,' I say, holding out my fist, already knowing it's a mistake. 'On three.'

'One, two, three,' we say together.

I hold out my hand, my eyes half closed and my fist still clenched. Emily strikes my knuckles with her open palm and squeals with excitement.

'Paper beats stone!' she says. 'It should be in a cabinet at the top of the stairs. But be quick about it, won't you?'

I scurry up the curved staircase. The light that managed to squeeze through the slit-thin windows on the ground floor barely follows me and by the time I reach the top, I'm smothered in darkness.

Fumbling around with outstretched arms, I feel something cold like glass. My eyes narrow. Then my fingers rest on a metal handle no bigger than a brass button. I give it a swift tug, but the damn thing won't budge.

'Emily!' I shout. 'I need those keys. I think the cabinet is locked.'

There's a second of silence, which seems to last an hour. Then her voice comes echoing back up the stairwell. 'Of course it's locked. Just smash it, we haven't got time to mess about.'

I pull my sleeve over my hand and draw back my arm. Then I hear the rattle of keys over my shoulder. 'Emily, is that you?'

'No, I'm still keeping watch,' she calls.

'Well, if it's not you, then who the hell is it?'

'It's Boris,' a gruff voice says from behind me.

Without a thought I smash my fist through the glass and grab the first thing that my hand finds. Then a large shadow appears at the top of the stairs, followed by a giant man with his shoulders hunched forward.

'Emily!' I scream. 'I need help up here.'

'Go up higher,' she shouts. 'There's a fire escape at the back. I'll meet you there.'

I run up another flight of steps, the jangle of keys chases from behind. There's a wide open space at the top, wooden benches line up along the walls and moonlight sprays through a window at the back, illuminating the whole room.

I glance up at the thick wooden roof trusses. A man hangs from a rope, a noose tightly shanked around his neck.

I walk towards him as he slowly unwinds, spinning around like a figurine on top of a music box.

Finally he comes to a halt, his face right in front of mine. Breath seeps from his open mouth and fogs the air, his skin is stone grey and his tongue hangs limply to one side. Then his eyes spring open.

'I hope he gives you a quick death,' he groans. 'Just pray he hasn't been on the bottle, so that your neck snaps cleanly when you fall.'

I pause for a moment, unable to take my eyes off him. Veins burst around his temples and his blackened feet point downwards like a ballerina. He's probably hung like that since the day he died, his soul tormented by his slow drawn-out death.

Then a hand rests on my shoulder and I realise that I'm about to be next.

My grip tightens around the heavy book. Holding it up to cover my face, I turn around and peep over the top to see a large hunchbacked man. His face is deformed, with one eye much lower than the other and a bulge protruding from his forehead.

'Nobody escapes Boris the Executioner,' he says, reaching over my shoulder to the man hanging from the ceiling and making him spin around again.

I take a step backwards and get tangled up in the hanged man's legs for a moment. Then I glance behind me. The large window at the back is surrounded by thick steel bars, set deeply into the stonework.

There's no chance of any escape.

Suddenly I see ten bony fingers appear on the window ledge, followed by a mass of fire-red hair and a pair of piercing green eyes.

'Rose, pass me the book,' Emily shouts. 'And hurry!'

I look back at Boris edging closer; the weight of the book is the only thing between us.

'I can help you,' cries Emily. 'But you need to pass me the book.'

She reaches one of her bony arms between the bars and places a hand on the cover. I look into her eyes, her pretty green eyes. Then I look back at Boris, with a set of keys twirling around in one hand and a thick length of rope trailing from the other.

I hand the book over to Emily and she just manages to squeeze it between the bars. Then she disappears out of sight.

Suddenly I feel exposed.

Now Boris is so close, I can feel his warm breath on my face. Emily's fingers reappear, wrapping themselves tightly around the steel bars.

Somehow her frail hands manage to prise the bars apart, making a wide enough gap for a person to squeeze through.

Her arms reach in and her grip tightens under my arms as she pulls me out onto the metal fire escape.

'Nobody escapes from Boris?' she laughs, as she helps me down onto a ladder.

Boris leans out after us, his thick frame far too wide to slip through the gap. 'You'll pay for this! I'll tie a rope to the roof beams with your name on it. It'll wait. But one day you'll pay.'

Emily gets to the bottom first; I'm at least three rungs behind when my foot slips off. My grip fades, my fingers unable to cling to the wet steel. Then my eyes fall shut.

When they finally open, I find myself resting safely in Emily's arms. She's holding me like a baby.

'How the hell did you get so strong?' I say.

'I will tell you,' Emily says, with urgency in her voice. 'But not right now.'

'Why not? After all you've put me through tonight, I think I've got a right to know.'

'You do,' she says, pointing to a crowd of torchlights heading our way. 'But not right now!'

We run around the front of the museum and race each other down Angel Hill. Emily pulls ahead, her satchel with her precious book in it swinging wildly. A mob of voices chases us from behind.

Emily bursts into the central square first, and I follow just half a stride behind.

'Damn it!' she screams. 'The abbey gates are locked.'

'Where now?' I gasp.

'We've got to make it to the chapel! It's the only safe place.'

'How? There's no way I'm climbing that wall again. Not after what happened to Scarlett.'

The crowd of monks are closing in on us. Their burning torches flood the central square, casting a flickering half-light that scrapes the walls of the old buildings.

'Follow me,' Emily says.

We run past the Norman Tower, past the traffic lights and over the first of the Humping Monks. 'Oh no!' Emily points across to the other side. 'It looks like we've got company.'

The monks have split forces and are surrounding us, slowly closing in from both sides of the Bream. 'Hold them here until he comes,' one of them shouts. 'He'll definitely want to talk to these two.'

Emily tugs on my sleeve, her eyes sharply jumping sideways over the walls of the bridge.

'You must be kidding,' I say.

Then a grinding sound jars across the square and the portcullis in the Norman Tower begins to rise, revealing a figure dressed in white.

'Over here!' the monks shout. 'We've got two of them here.'

With that Emily leaps off the side of the bridge, dragging me with her. My body strikes the water. A sharp pain like a thousand daggers pierces my skin. My head goes under and a burning fills my lungs.

I bob back up to the surface, scanning wildly for Emily. But she's nowhere to be seen. My head goes under again and I'm swept through a tunnel that breaches the abbey walls.

'Come on!' Emily says, as I emerge on the other side.

'Help!' I shout. 'I can't swim.'

My clothes are filled with water, their weight like a giant hand dragging me under. Emily appears beside me, her wet hair welded to her face. She tightens her arm around my neck, almost stopping my breath. Then she pulls me along on my back.

The chattering of voices disappears in the distance. I look up at the sky, with the Bream lapping over my chin. Foul-tasting water hits the back of my throat. I try to cough it up, but it makes things worse, my open mouth taking in more and more.

The little wooden footbridge that joins the graveyard to the orchard appears overhead, blocking out my view of the stars. That's the last thing I see. Then everything turns black.

– You Know What I Am –

I wake to the crackle of firewood. A thick plume of
smoke rises before me. My wet clothes are sprawled out
on the ground, and I've got Emily's sackcloth dress
draped around my shoulders for warmth.

A gust of wind stokes the flames and clears my line
of sight. Standing by the fire is the silhouette of a young
woman. But somehow she no longer looks like the
scrawny teenager I woke up a couple nights ago. Her
red hair has dried into a frizz and the tender light of the
fire caresses her hourglass figure. Her breasts are full,
sitting firm either side of the leather strap of her satchel
as she dances naked around the blaze.

'What happened?' I say, dazed. 'Where are we?'

'We're on the island outside the chapel,' Emily says.
'We're safe here.'

'Give me my clothes. I want to go home.'

'You can't. Even if you could get off the island,
you'd never make it across the Bream. I did something
to stop anyone crossing until sunrise.'

'You did what?' I say. 'And what happened to the
monks?'

'I can only answer one question at a time,' she says,
pulling the book out of her leather bag and passing it
my way. 'Everything you need to know is in here.'

I stroke my hand across the cover, feeling its texture.
'Somehow it's still dry. By rights it should be soaked
through. I saw you swim with it down the river.'

'But it's not made from paper.'

'Then what is it made from?'

'The cover is leather,' Emily replies. 'And the pages, they're made from human skin.'

I throw the book hard onto the ground. As it lies there deeply set into the mud, I notice a five-pointed star on the cover, glistening in gold leaf.

'You bent the bars in the museum with your bare hands. You said that you did something to the river and now look at you,' I say. 'You suddenly look like a…'

'Like a what?' Emily says.

I pause a while as she slowly strides towards me. Her hands reach out and gently stroke my cheeks.

'You know what I am,' she says, sliding her hand around the back of my neck and pulling me to my feet.

We stand there, our bare chests pushed together as the sackcloth dress slips off my shoulders and falls to the ground. A cold gust of wind sends a shiver down my back, but Emily's body burns against me, her pretty green eyes staring deeply into mine.

'You know what I am,' she whispers into my ear. 'Say it, I dare you…'

'You're a witch,' I scream, trying to push her away. 'You lied to me, you're a witch!'

'That's right,' she says, pressing her soft lips against mine and then smiling. 'But I never lied to you. We *were* the Sisters of Burnham All-Saints Chapel, we *were* killed for our beliefs. But times were hard back then. Everybody had two jobs if they wanted to survive. We were nuns by day and witches by night.'

'Don't make a joke of it. You lied to me. You used me to get that book,' I say. 'And now look at you standing there in the cold of night. You look…'

'Powerful,' Emily says. 'Powerful enough to wake up my sisters and together we'll be powerful enough to wake up yours. That bit is true, I swear.'

Finally I force my body free and cover myself with the sackcloth dress. I stare at Emily, who is stooping down to pick up the book, clearly unashamed about being naked in front of me.

'This book is made from the skin of my dead sisters,' she says. 'It holds more than just their stories; within its pages are their souls. If we take it to the place where they were killed and rest it on the Earth, their spirits will be awoken. One by one we will take them here to the mausoleum. That will be their final resting place and then I'll join them on the other side. Together we will find your sister Scarlett and send her back. You have to believe me, Rose; please, you have to help.'

My heart feels like it might burst out of my chest. What she says sounds so far-fetched – but I saw her bend the steel bars. All I can think of is Scarlett laying helplessly in bed, and the doctors saying that there's nothing that can be done and trying to convince Mum to turn off her life-support.

'Okay,' I say. 'I'll help. But I'm doing it for Scarlett, not for you.'

'For our sisters, then.' Emily pulls a bottle out from her satchel. 'Let's drink to our sisters!'

'You told me there was no vodka in your plan tonight,' I say.

'I told you that I would try. But I didn't promise.'

There's a long pause and then we both laugh.

'To our sisters,' I shout, snatching the bottle from her hand and taking a swig.

We huddle around the fire drinking vodka through the small hours of the morning. Together we flick through the pages of Emily's book. Although I can barely read it in the dark, Emily explains to me how each page tells the story of how one of her sisters was tried and executed for the crime of witchcraft.

'Who would do such a thing?' I ask.

'He called himself the Witch-Hunter,' Emily replies. 'He was a religious man from the abbey. He was always dressed in white.'

'Like the one chasing us tonight? Like Father Parfitt?'

'No, he was much younger. Besides, it was over three hundred years ago, it couldn't have been your history teacher.'

'But there's something not right about him,' I say. 'I swear I saw him surrounded by dead monks last night. Are you sure we're safe here? As far as I know he only lives at the rectory just behind the chapel.'

'The last time you saw him he was on the other side of the Bream, wasn't he?' Emily asks. 'Coming out of the Norman Tower?'

'I guess so.'

'Then dead or alive, history teacher or witch-hunter, he can't cross the river until morning.'

'How can you be so sure?'

'Because together with the spirit of my sisters, I harnessed the power of the moon,' Emily says. 'That's where witches draw their strength from. From the Earth, from the Moon, from Mother Nature herself. There's nothing evil about us. You do believe me, don't you?'

I look at her, the firelight catching those pretty eyes of hers.

'I do believe you,' I say. 'After all, you could have deserted me in the museum to face the executioner or even left me alone to fight off the monks.'

The fire begins to wane as the sun slowly pulls its head over the horizon. An amber blanket spreads across the land where the light meets the morning mist. It nestles around the chapel and then gently wafts across the lake, warming the wet grass between my toes.

'Pass me my clothes,' I say. 'I think it's time I was going.'

'Once morning arrives the dead will rest,' Emily says. 'Just beware of the history teacher; we still don't know what *he* is.'

'Don't worry, I can outrun him. As long as he's alone.'

'I'll see you again tomorrow, then.' Emily holds out her palm. 'We've got a whole coven of sisters to wake up.'

'Usual time, usual place,' I say, shaking her hand.

She helps me onto a little wooden raft that's been hidden amongst the reeds. Once I'm aboard, she sits down on the shore and launches me off with her feet. She waits until I'm almost across and then she waves me goodbye.

'Remember to watch out for the man in white,' she calls. Then she disappears inside the mausoleum.

– Billy Has Lost the Plot –

A bright sun rises in the graveyard, painting the tufts of grass silver as it reflects off the morning dew. I hurry across the Bream, the sound of birds sing from the trees and leaves rustle beneath my feet. Squirrels scurry across the forest floor, foraging for food amongst the thicket, and just for a moment, I feel at ease.

I realise that as morning overpowers night, the dead rest and the living rise.

I slow down in a clearing of trees and glance up at the cathedral. The grounds-men have arrived early and are raking leaves away from the vestry. They distract me for a moment. Then something strikes me hard on the shin, tripping me to the ground.

I stand up and wipe myself down, discovering that I've stumbled on a single headstone. It looks so miserable, planted there alone, away from the graveyard. For some reason it draws me in and I crouch beside it to see what's written on it.

In memory of Billy Tanner,
1834-1853,
A loving son forever missed.

My eyes mist up with tears. Poor Billy, I know he must have died young, but still it seems so sad to see his name written there in faded writing. I clear away the worst of the leaves, waiting for the workmen to finish at the back of the vestry. Then I scurry up the hill and steal a rose from the cathedral garden. I place it beside Billy's grave and sit there for a moment, paying my respects.

There's a loud boom and the church bells chime eight. It means the abbey gate must be open and even if old Parfitt is about, there's no way he would try anything in daylight. So I pick myself up and run towards the central square, worried whether Mum will have noticed that I've been out all night.

When I arrive home, I see that Bluebell is missing from the front of the house. It's a good sign. There's no way Mum would have left for work if she knew I wasn't home.

I go straight through the front door and into the hallway, where the woodchip walls are covered in photos of Scarlett. There's one of her and Jack on the night of the lower sixth-form ball. If you really look hard you can just see me somewhere, hiding in the background. I didn't mind. To be honest, I never liked the way I look in photos.

Unlike Scarlett, if she wasn't taking *selfies* on her phone, then she was pestering everybody to take her picture, even strangers in the street. At the time it used to make me so embarrassed, but right now I'd do anything to take another photo of her, whilst she whines about catching her best side or getting the right light.

I wander into the kitchen and take a look on the table. There's no snotty note or anything, just yesterday's burnt toast still lying on the table and a pile of dirty plates in the sink. Mum must have just got up and gone without checking on me first. It's no surprise really. She knows not to wake me up, not unless she wants a row. But not clearing up, that's not like her. And we've barely spoken in days.

I'm starting to worry about her.

I stagger upstairs and into my room; my unmade bed looks so warm and inviting. If I really hurry, I might just be able to make the second bell. But then again, it's only Thursday, which means English in the morning, followed by general studies in the afternoon.

Really, who the hell cares about general studies?

I get up around mid-afternoon and give the kitchen a once-over to help Mum out. When she gets home, it's off to see Scarlett again, but there's no progress on that front. The doctor spends less than a couple of minutes at Scarlett's bedside with us; then he takes Mum off to his office for another one of their *secret* meetings.

Even on the way home we don't say more than a couple of words to each other. Mum looks as if she has the worries of the world swirling around her head and all I can think about is joining up with Emily and getting started with our plan.

When we get back, Mum runs herself a bath and then she's straight off to bed. Five minutes later, I'm pulling on a black hooded top and I'm out the back gate into Saint Mary's Walks.

It's a little before midnight when I arrive in the central square and Emily is nowhere to be seen. It's far from cold for the time of year and mild air from this morning's sun has misted up the sky, like a warm breath on cold glass.

The portcullis of the Norman Tower is closed as usual, but I daren't wait outside, just in case old Parfitt is lurking about. So I stroll across the Humping Monks to kill some time, keeping watch for Emily from a distance.

'Psst! Under here,' a voice cries.

I look down at the towpath that runs along the Bream. There's nothing to see; even the water looks still, gently shimmering under the streetlights.

'Under here!' the voice says again.

I run down the steps and there, hiding beneath the Humping Monks, is Emily, dressed in her tatty sackcloth dress with her beloved book hanging out of the top of her satchel.

'I thought you said to meet at the normal place,' I say.

'From now on this is the normal place,' Emily replies. 'With your friend the history teacher wandering about, it's not safe for us outside the abbey.'

'It seems that sisters think alike.' I stretch out my arms and give her a hug. 'So how have you been? Have you worked out who you want to wake up first?'

'You know, I haven't thought about anything else since last night,' Emily says, grinning broadly. 'I think

94

we should start with Evelyn and Madelyn, the twins. That way we'll kill two birds with one stone.'

'So what's the plan? Have we got to take that book of yours to where they died?'

'You learn fast,' Emily says, smiling. 'We'll make a sister out of you yet.'

'So, where did they die?'

'Where were they murdered, do you mean?' Emily bares her teeth angrily. 'The son of a bitch drowned them out at Westbrook Wash. Have you heard of it?'

'The Bream runs through a village called Westbrook,' I say. 'But that's fifteen miles from here. And even if we had a car, with all the rain we've had recently, it's most probably flooded. It's really flat around that way, nothing more than fenland.'

'That's why we're going to need a boat. We'll have to jump on board the next one that comes past. Then mug the owners and throw them into the river.'

'Steady on. Maybe Billy can help us.'

'Billy?' Emily says. 'This isn't any of his business, it's for our sisters.'

'But the other night he told me that his old man was coming into the Dry Dock. He said he was going to meet him there too. He's got a boat and everything.'

'All this happened hundreds of years ago, Rose, what makes you think he'd still be there? Besides, we don't even know what he looks like.'

'Yeah, but Billy does.'

'But Billy isn't here, is he?'

'I know, but I found his tombstone in the cathedral orchard this morning. It said in loving memory of a beloved son.'

'I still don't know where you're going with this, Rose,' Emily says.

'You said it yourself, most of the dead are harmless, just going about their business until they put their souls to rest. Well, I'm ready to bet that Billy never made it to the Dry Dock. I reckon he died in the One-Eyed Monk and that's why his old man left that writing on his tombstone.'

'And if that's true,' Emily says, 'then his old man is most probably still wandering the Earth looking for him.'

'Or still at the Dry Dock.'

Just then there's a rumble like thunder and it feels as if the bridge is about to cave in.

'What the hell was that?' Emily asks.

'Maybe it's Billy coming in on that milk wagon, on his way to the One-Eye,' I say, grabbing her by the sleeve.

We run up the steps onto street level and sure enough there's Billy, standing outside the abbey gate, tipping his cap and whistling to the driver to pull away.

'Billy!' I shout. 'Over here!'

He comes bowling over with a swagger to his stride. 'If it isn't my two favourite ladies,' he says, grinning. 'Fancy another visit to the One-Eye?'

'No Billy,' I say. 'I've got something to tell you, something important.'

'You can't be pregnant. I know we were drunk and I can't remember how we got home, but we never even kissed, we couldn't have… Not the three of us!'

'No Billy, we didn't,' I say.

'And trust me, we couldn't have,' Emily adds.

'Look Billy,' I say, grabbing his arm. 'I found your grave in the cathedral orchard this morning. I've got a feeling you died at the One-Eyed Monk, many years ago. And I reckon your old man's been waiting for you at the Dry Dock ever since.'

'What the hell have you been drinking?' Billy laughs. 'I told you, he'll be in tomorrow.'

'Yes, Billy. But that was two nights ago.'

Billy stops laughing and his face turns cold. 'So it was.'

'Come on, Billy,' Emily says, sticking out her new womanly chest in his direction. 'Come and join us ladies for a moonlight stroll up the river. If we're wrong, then you can always take us down the One-Eye afterwards and show us the night of our lives again.'

'Well, when you put it like that,' Billy says, taking us each by the arm. 'How can I resist?'

We tread the towpath for a mile or more, following the Bream as she slithers across furrowed fields that lay barren for the winter. The church bells faintly chime one, and a moment later the clock tower falls below the horizon and the night swallows the last remaining lights of Burnham.

'It feels like we've been walking forever,' I say. 'How much further?'

'Not far,' Billy says. 'You should see the Dry Dock any moment now.'

We come to a row of brightly painted narrow boats, their candle-lights gently melting through the mist and reflecting off the river. The boats are lined up for what must be a hundred yards or more, sometimes two and three abreast, leading towards a large rotting boatshed which juts out into the water on a pair of wooden stilts.

'There she is,' Billy says, pointing ahead. 'Dad said that you have to get there real early if you want a drink. That's why they call it the Dry Dock. It seems the more time you spend on the water, the thirstier you get.'

'What did you say your Dad's boat was called, Billy?' I say. 'There's got to be twenty or thirty of them here, at least.'

'The Plot,' Billy says. 'We're looking for the Plot.'

Emily steps onto the first boat without a care of who it might belong to and whether they would mind. 'Nope, this one is called Lavender. Your turn, Rose.'

I tiptoe towards the next one, which has another boat pulled alongside it. 'I can't see a name. It's too dark.'

'Maybe it's on the far side?' Billy says. 'Jump on board and have a look.'

'Do I have to?'

'It was your idea,' Billy says. 'If it wasn't for you, I'd be in the One-Eye by now, with a beer in my hand and a lady on my lap.'

I step aboard and the boat gently sways before crashing into the one it's moored to. I spot a sign on the second boat, just above a row of small round windows that are almost submerged beneath the water. Stretching out my arms, I hold myself across the gap to get a better look.

'This one's called The Lovebirds,' I say.

Then the face of an old lady appears against one of the portholes. 'Ned, wake up!' she cries. 'Grab your shotgun too. It looks like we're being turned over!'

The two boats begin to drift apart, forcing me to fall forward. Staring down into the dark brown depths of the Bream, I'm stretched out between them like a rope ladder. My arms are pulled from their sockets and one of my feet slips over the edge and dangles into the water.

'Help!' I scream. 'Help! I can't swim.'

Billy leaps on board and pulls on the back of my hood, reeling me in like a soggy piece of rope. 'That was close,' he says, as we lie there in a heap back on the first boat. 'You should have said that you couldn't swim.'

'Would it have made a difference?' I say, my lips just a few inches away from his.

'What have we got here?' a voice says from above.

I look up. Billy and I are staring down the barrels of a shotgun. A tall wiry man looms over us, dressed in a pair of dirty white long-johns and a string vest that has seen better days. A shiver runs up the knotted veins of his legs, resonating at his finger which rests on the trigger.

'What are you doing on my boat?' he says in a high-pitched squeal. 'Speak now or forever hold your peace!'

'Young lovers, lost in the night,' Billy says quickly, and then he kisses me passionately on the lips.

I pull away to see the old man smiling. 'Now that takes me back,' he says, lowering the tone of his voice, along with his gun. 'Sneaking around in the small hours of the night, all in the hope of getting lucky.'

Just then a second voice comes booming across form the other boat. 'Ned! What on God's Earth is going on?'

It's the old woman I saw through the porthole. She's wrapped up warm in a thick fur coat, making her look twice the size of Ned. And if her gruff voice is anything to go by, she sounds twice as cruel.

'Ned. I can hear too much talking and not enough shooting,' she says.

'Don't worry, my little honeybee. It's just a couple of young lovers, lost their way in the dark.' Ned leans on his shotgun, which is now faced down to the floor. 'It reminds me of us, all those years ago.'

'Oh Neddy, you're such a sweetie,' the old woman says. 'Now blow their bloody brains out and come to bed with me.'

Ned raises his shotgun back from the deck and takes aim. His left eye closes, his grip tightens around the butt. 'I'm sorry, but if that's how my honeybee wants it…' he says.

Just then Emily jumps from the shadows and strikes the old lady clean on the head with her satchel. The woman falls to the floor, but Emily continues to hit her.

'For God's sake shut your bloody mouth,' Emily says. 'Take that, you fat old bitch!'

Ned turns in their direction and lets off a wayward shot into the air. The gun recoils into his shoulder, sending him off balance. Billy sees his chance and grabs Ned's ankle, pushing his foot over the side. Ned falls into the water and winds up wedged between the two boats. One of his hands is still gripped around the gun and he's waving it around wildly in the air.

'Pull on the other side,' Billy shouts to me, grabbing a piece of rope at the bow. 'Haul the boats together.'

I roll over and heave on its moorings at the stern. Old Ned's head bobs up between the two barges; his grip loosens around his shotgun and it falls onto the deck. I see his face, twisting with pain as Billy and I squeeze the breath from his lungs.

Emily kicks the old woman overboard. Then she grabs Ned's shotgun and begins to bludgeon his head with the blunt end.

'How do you like that?' she says. 'How does your own gun taste?'

Ned disappears into the Bream and I fall back onto the boat exhausted.

'For heaven's sake, Emily!' I shout. 'Did you have to?'

'He was going to blow your head off, Rose,' Emily says. 'I thought you'd be grateful.'

'Billy could have talked him round. I know he could.'

'And what if he hadn't? They're ghosts, Rose, they're already dead. They'll be right back here again this time tomorrow.'

'But did you have to laugh while you did it?'

'I did what I had to,' Emily says. 'For my sisters.'

There's a long pause as Billy comes over and puts an arm around me. 'She's right, Rose,' he says. 'Me and Emily, we're already dead. But you, you've got your whole life ahead of you. We couldn't take that chance with you.'

'Listen to your boyfriend, Rose,' Emily says, picking up her satchel. 'I'm going to check on these other boats, to see if any of them are called the Plot.'

Billy and I sit there awhile on the deck of Ned's boat and share each other's warmth. Candlelight gently smudges across the water like an oil painting. The wind whistles along the Bream and the gentle swaying of the boat slowly returns my breathing to normal.

'Emily was only looking out for you, Rose,' Billy says. 'I'd have done the same.'

'Yes, but you wouldn't have laughed like she did,' I say. 'There are things you don't know about her, Billy. She's not all sweetness and light.'

'I know. But she'd do anything for you. She looks at you as a sister.'

'She's not my sister,' I say. 'She's nothing like Scarlett.'

There's a strained silence as the Bream laps its way between the two boats and softly kisses them together. My stomach churns. My head is filled with thoughts about Scarlett and what I'd do to see her eyes open and full of life. Truth be told, I've got no idea if Billy's Dad is really waiting around here for us. I just want to get my hands on his boat.

I guess Emily and I aren't that different after all.

'I hope you didn't mind me kissing you?' Billy says, interrupting my lonely thoughts.

'Not at all,' I say, laughing. 'But I only kissed you back because that man was holding a shotgun to my head.'

'Oh, is that right?' Billy says, grinning broadly. 'Just you looked like you enjoyed it to me.'

'Did I now? I thought a man like you, in your hundreds of years of experience, might have learnt to tell when a girl is faking it, Billy.'

'Oh, I've learnt,' Billy says, tenderly stroking my face and slowly moving his lips towards mine. 'They never fake it with me.'

There's a loud cough from behind. 'I hope I'm not interrupting anything,' Emily says. 'But I've been as a far as the Dry Dock and there isn't a boat called the Plot anywhere.'

'Sorry, Billy,' I say, with his lips almost touching mine. 'What are we going to do?'

'Well, why don't you two lovebirds get cosy on Ned's boat here and I'll take his *honeybee's* boat and go and look for my sisters,' Emily says, folding her arms sharply.

'Look, we've come this far,' Billy says. 'We should at least check out the Dry Dock. If there's nobody there, then we'll all go and look for your sisters together.'

'If we must.' Emily picks up Ned's shotgun and wedges it beneath the strap of her satchel. 'But you're really slowing me down with all that smooching. So give it a rest, won't you?'

A blustering wind picks up, making the rotting boat shed groan on its stilts. The pitched roof on top bends and sways; one more big gust looks like it could blow the whole place down at any moment. The only door appears to be up on the jetty and the only way up seems to be via a rickety ladder, with half of its rungs either broken or missing.

'Ladies first,' Billy says, holding out a hand to help Emily up onto the first step.

'Nice try,' Emily says. 'You just want get a look up my skirt when I'm climbing.'

'Why?' Billy says smiling. 'Have you got those nice frilly knickers on again?'

'Again?' Emily snarls, punching him hard on the upper arm. 'That's for me to know and you *never* to find out!'

Billy laughs before making his way up the ladder, followed by Emily. By the time I'm up at the top, they've already been greeted by an old man sweeping the deck. He looks at least a hundred years old. His back is bent, hunched over a broom that is probably holding him up as much as he's holding it.

'We're closed for the night,' he says. 'We're out of hot food and almost out of beer too.'

'That's alright,' Billy says. 'We were just looking for a boat.'

'Boats are down there on the water,' the old man says. 'There's just me and some old drunk fella up here. In fact, I'll stand you a pint for the road if you help me shift him. He's been drinking the place dry. Between you and me, I don't think he's all there. He says it himself. He's lost the plot.'

'He said what?' Billy says.

'He says he's lost the plot,' the old man replies. 'He says he's lost the plot.'

– Goodbye Billy –

Billy barges open the door and we all step inside, leaving the old man to finish sweeping the deck. The Dry Dock is a high-ceilinged building that looks like it's made from giant matchsticks. Candlelight licks its way up the walls, leading to exposed studwork that is cobbled together with rusty nails.

A long bar runs the length of the room, with big empty saucepans at one end and barrels of beer at the other. Sitting alone in the far corner is a scruffy-looking man. His trousers are torn, and his flat-cap crumpled and laid on the table next to an empty pint glass.

'Dad, is that you?' Billy runs on ahead of us.

'I've been called many things in my time,' the man replies, slurring his words. 'But I can't remember the last time someone called me that.'

'Dad, it's me. It's Billy.'

'My Billy?' the man says, struggling to his feet. 'It can't be. My Billy is just a boy, just a little boy. My Billy is...'

'Dead,' Billy says, throwing out his arms and squeezing the man tightly.

They sway back and forth, knocking Billy's hat clean off his head. As they let go, the family resemblance becomes clear. The old man might have less hair and a few more wrinkles on his brow, but as a smile stretches across his face, the same mischievous sparkle lights up in his eyes.

'Well, aren't you going to introduce me to your girlfriends then, boy?' he says. 'Which one's mine?'

'This is Rose and that's Emily,' Billy says. 'It's because of Rose that I found you.'

'So I'll take the one with the pretty eyes and the big chest,' Billy's dad says. 'I always did like a redhead.'

'Lay a finger on me and I'll blow your brains out,' Emily replies, taking Ned's shotgun down off her shoulder and pointing it in his face.

'God help me, I've died and gone to heaven,' Billy's dad says excitedly. 'I do like a woman who can stand up for herself.'

'Talking of which,' Billy says. 'How's my Ma?'

'Oh, Billy,' his dad says, his voice cracking a little. 'Your mum is finally resting, along with your sisters. It must be a hundred and fifty years or more since I saw her. She never did forgive me for not bringing you home.'

'Maybe we can see her? Together.'

'Of course we can, Billy. Your mum will be made up.' His dad says, wiping a tear from his eye. 'But first we've got to thank these girls for bringing you home. A round of drinks for the road!'

'We haven't got time,' Emily says. 'But there is something you could do if you want to thank us.'

'Anything. I owe you the world and everything in it, for bringing me back my boy.'

'Billy said you had a boat. We need to get up to Westbrook Wash.'

107

'A boat? She's a little more than just a boat.'

With that we head out of the Dry Dock and out onto the jetty. The old man sweeping the deck waves us past and we hurry down the ladder. 'Thank God for that,' he says. 'Oh and take your bloody boat with you.'

Billy's dad walks around the back of the boatshed and ushers us through a stable door on the ground floor. Moored up under the cover of the jetty is the grandest boat I've ever seen. The hull is painted in a Bordeaux shade of red, sat below a sumptuous black cabin. Polished brass portholes run along its length and then, in the most intricate of gold lettering, the words *Tanner and Son* are written down the side.

'Gor blimey, Dad!' Billy says. 'She's everything you said she was in your letter and more.'

'Yeah, she's a good ship, ladies. None of this horse-towed rubbish. Get a good head of steam on her and there isn't a boat on the river that can keep up with her.'

'Why are you telling us?' I say. 'Aren't you coming?'

'No,' Billy's dad says. 'Me and the boy are heading in the other direction.'

'Are you sure, Mr Tanner?' I say, throwing my arms around him. 'We'll take good care of her.'

'I've got no need for her anymore. Oh and check the hold. It's full of women's clothes that me and Billy were going to sell on the market. Pick yourselves out something pretty and think of us, won't you.'

'We sure will,' Emily says excitedly, jumping aboard and disappearing into the cabin.

There's an awkward pause for a moment. For once even Billy seems lost for something to say.

'Well, I guess this is goodbye,' I say, taking the initiative.

'No. It's just goodbye for now,' Billy says, kissing me softly on the cheek. 'One day, I'll see you on the other side.'

'One day, Billy, many years from now,' I say. 'But if you come across a prettier version of me called Scarlett on your travels, then send her home, won't you?'

'That's impossible,' Billy says, with that playful look in his eye. 'She couldn't be any prettier than you.'

'Oh, Billy," I say, stepping onto the Plot. 'What am I going to do without you?'

I look back over my shoulder and time stands still for a moment, until Emily appears through a trapdoor on the bridge. She's wearing an olive haute-neck dress, made from the finest silk, that hugs her figure right down to the floor. It really suits her, set against the colour of her hair and matching her bright green eyes.

She blows the horn and then gently pushes down a big brass lever, steering the Plot from under the jetty. We drift out onto the river, with Billy and his dad waving us off before they slowly disappear into the mist. Then I join Emily up on the bridge.

'Can you believe it?' she says. 'Our own boat and new clothes too.'

'I know, you look amazing. It's a bit nicer than that old sackcloth dress of yours.'

'Do you think?' She manages to keep a straight face for a couple of seconds before a smile creeps through.

Casually holding the giant steering wheel in one hand, she eases the Plot along the Bream. Waves lick alongside us, whilst the lantern at the front gently gnaws through the mist. Fresh air fills my lungs and the feel of the wind rushes beneath my hood. There's something special about travelling along the water at night; something peaceful that makes your troubles seem more distant.

'Hey, I'm sorry about earlier,' Emily says. 'Maybe I did go too far with Ned and his wife.'

'Don't worry about it. You did it for your sisters.'

'For *our* sisters,' she says, putting her arm around me.

'Yes, for our sisters.' I lean my head onto her shoulder.

The river begins to widen. The bank becomes littered with dying shrubs, their exposed roots like rotting veins, decaying in the water. The land beyond them flattens and a few lights melt their way through the mist in the distance. Still I can't make out any buildings, but I do get the feeling that we're approaching civilisation of some sort.

'Maybe we're here?' Emily says. 'You did say that the Bream runs right through Westbrook.'

'So what now?' I ask. 'Surely we can't lay your book down on the riverbed.'

'I'll find something to moor up against and we'll have a look around on foot.' Emily heaves back on the brass lever, slowing the Plot down. 'If worst comes to the worst, we'll take the book to the place where they pulled their bodies out of the river. We need to draw power from the Earth.'

– Evelyn and Madelyn –

The Plot drops to half steam and we slowly chug towards the riverbank. I jump down onto the deck, tying us up against a tree. Then I unhook the lantern from the bow and wait for Emily to join me. Slowly she clambers down from the bridge, clutching her beloved book in one hand and daintily lifting her long flowing skirt off the floor with the other.

I don't know why she bothers, though, because the moment we step ashore we're up to our ankles in a black peaty soil that smells of rotten vegetables.

'Mum's going to kill me when she sees the state of my jeans,' I say. 'And what about your new dress?'

'Don't worry. There's plenty more in the hold. We'll all pick out something else together, just as soon as we find the twins.'

She bends down and tears off the bottom of her dress, so that it barely comes halfway down her thighs. 'That's better,' she laughs. 'After all, we both know now that I'm a witch and not a nun.'

We struggle on arm in arm and as soon as we get a few yards from the riverbank, the ground becomes firmer. Spurred on by the lights of Westbrook burning through the mist, we pick up an old bridle path that runs parallel to the Bream. It's lined with tall trees; their lifeless branches rake the ground beneath them. They look completely dead; there aren't even any leaves lying around their roots.

'I get the feeling nothing grows here anymore,' Emily says, scanning around as if she's looking for something in particular. 'It's like the ground is scarred.'

We follow the path for a hundred yards or more, until the trees begin to thin out. In the middle of the clearing, I spot an ivy-infested wall, no higher than my waist. It's circled around two weathered posts, which barely hold up a red slate roof. Although it must have been standing here for a few hundred years, it slouches sideways and by the look of things a well-placed kick could bring down the whole thing in a matter of seconds.

Suddenly Emily goes still.

'What's wrong?' I ask.

'We're here,' she says. 'This is where it happened.'

'How can you be so sure?'

'It's not something you can forget that easily. Not even after three hundred years. Hidden in this well, this is where I saw him murder my sisters.'

'How did he…?'

'Sit,' Emily says, taking the lantern from my hand and laying her book out on the ground between us.

She opens the cover of the thick leather tome, turning the pages until she finds the right one. 'May 1st 1692,' she says, her voice shaking a little as she reads. 'Evelyn and Madelyn Cullender, of Burnham All-Saints Chapel, executed for the crime of witchcraft.'

She pauses awhile, her eyes glistening with tears. 'The pair were first suspected of bringing the devil

113

amongst the good people of Burnham All-Saints when they were seen attempting to buy herrings in the market square on the morning of April 16th 1692. They were refused the right of purchase and three days later the stall holders fell ill.'

'That was it?' I say. 'That was all they did?'

'There's more.' Emily turns the page. 'Upon further investigation, it was discovered the pair had kept the company of numerous men, some of whom were married and of local notoriety. The pair appeared at Suffolk County Court on April 29th 1692, in accordance with the Act of Witchcraft 1602, where they received a trial by ordeal. Upon holding a burning iron for the count of ten, both received wounds to their palms. As God would surely come to the aid of the innocent, the accused were assumed guilty of witchcraft.'

'That's insane,' I say. 'Absolute madness...'

'Their wounds were dressed and checked again, but had not healed by sunrise of May 1st 1692. This supported a verdict of guilt. The accused were then taken to Westbrook Wash and bound to a tree for the duration of the day, where they were offered the opportunity to confess, in exchange for death by hanging. As neither had confessed by sunset, they were sentenced to ordeal by water and eventually drowned during the night.'

'What the hell is ordeal by water?' I ask.

'It's the most cowardly thing that I've ever seen.' By now Emily has tears streaming down her face. 'He stripped them bare and walked them to the water's edge, the old men with him all leering at their naked flesh. The others and I could see it all from just inside this well. Then he bound their arms and legs behind their backs and cast them into the river. We couldn't watch any longer; we ran out and tried to stop it. But there were too many of them. I remember him grabbing me, the one in white. He was so strong, unnaturally strong. That's how the rest of us were caught.'

'Why didn't you use magic on them?' I say. 'Draw strength from the moon and stop them crossing the river or something?'

'That needs at least six sisters touching each other and it takes time. We got split up in the fighting. Like I said, there were too many of them.'

'Did he drown you too?'

'No,' Emily says, her tears turning to laughter for a moment. 'We each got a *fair* trial of our own, a few days later.'

'It's alright,' I say, wiping her moist cheeks with my thumb. 'We're here now. We can bring them back and take them home to the chapel.'

'I know. It's just that sitting here I can see it so clearly,' Emily says, turning the book face down to the ground. 'It's almost as if it happened yesterday.'

'So what now? Should we get closer to the water?'

'No,' Emily replies. 'Here is perfect. The water beneath the well must run right out into the river where they died. We can channel its energy.'

We both sit cross-legged, our palms resting on the cover of the book, touching at the fingertips. The wind begins to rush through the corridor of trees, stirring the loose sticks and stones and clearing away the mist. Storm clouds brew overhead and the sky becomes varicose with thunder.

'Now repeat after me,' Emily says. 'I channel the Earth in the name of my sisters. Air, soil, water and fire, let my sisters wake.'

We say it together, over and over.

The sky becomes angry, seething full of energy. The clouds burst and lash down rain that soaks my hair, sticking it to my face. Small twigs are lifted from the ground and swirl around us, dancing in the air. Then a fork of lightning strikes the Bream.

'Sorores in Aeternum!' Emily screams.

Everything goes quiet. The storm blows over as swiftly as it arrived and the rain stops. A waxing moon now dominates the clear sky, high amongst a galaxy of stars. Beneath its silver glow a pair of silhouettes appear at the riverbank. Two girls, stark naked, with flowing locks of golden hair.

'Emily, is that you?' the girls say together, using exactly the same words at the same time.

'Who else?' Emily replies, running over to them. 'I told you I would save you. I told you.'

The three of them embrace, joining hands in a circle and then dancing at the water's edge. They chant in an ancient language, whilst I stand there holding up the

116

lantern. Steam curls off the naked bodies of the twins, which glisten in the half-light. Finally they stop dancing and line up along the riverbank, with Emily in the middle.

'Who's that with you?' the girl on her right asks.

'This is Rose,' Emily replies. 'She's one of us now.'

'Come join the circle,' the other girl says.

'I'd rather you put some clothes on first,' I say, slowly walking over.

'You initiated her yet?' the one on the right says. 'Maybe we should throw her into the river?'

'You'll do nothing of the sort,' Emily says. 'If it weren't for Rose, none of us would be here.'

'Don't mind her anyway,' the other twin says, laughing wildly. 'She's Evelyn, but I call her *Eviltwin*.'

'And she's Madelyn,' her sister says. 'But I call her *Madtwin*.'

I look them both up and down. Their naked bodies are still wet, but they don't seem the slightest bit cold or ashamed. They're both tall, wide-eyed, with perfect skin as pale as porcelain. To me, even up close, they look completely identical.

'Don't worry,' they both say together, as if they've read my mind. 'Once you get to know us, you'll soon be able to tell the difference.'

It makes me laugh.

'Do you always say the same thing, at the same time?' I ask.

'Not always,' Madelyn says.

'Sometimes we just finish off each other's sentences,' Evelyn adds.

Together we trudge back up the bridle path towards the Plot. Once we get on board it's straight below deck to get warm. We gather in a long galley-shaped room, with wooden panelled walls. Two oak benches sit on either side, lavishly upholstered in bright red fabric, just a few feet from a wrought-iron furnace.

Emily stokes the waning flame and then turns everyone's attention to a large cupboard at the far end. She opens the door and out spills a mountain of clothes onto the floor. There are long flowing dresses, feather bowers, frilly bras and knickers, and brightly coloured hats. The twins shriek in excitement and all of a sudden we're like a bunch of little girls playing with a dressing-up box.

'We should all have one of these,' Emily says, holding up a brown fur coat lined with dark green silk. 'It should be our thing.'

'I think I'll pass,' I say. 'I've got to go back into the twenty-first century later and nobody wears fur anymore. In fact, people throw paint over you if it's real.'

It doesn't stop the twins though. They dive into the jumble of clothes and both come out tugging at the same stripy grey jacket, which is probably made out of mink.

Madelyn eventually wins and slips it on straight over her naked body.

'That's typical of you,' Evelyn says, folding her arms. 'A fur coat with no knickers, that's what got us in all this trouble in the first place.'

'Well, I don't know why you're looking all high and mighty,' Madelyn replies. 'The only reason you wear knickers is to keep your ankles warm!'

'Both of you cut it out,' Emily says, trying to bring them to order. 'Now I remember why I waited three hundred years to wake you up.'

But her words have no effect and the pair continue to bicker like two babies at bath time.

Emily drags me up the stairs and closes the hatch on the bridge for good measure. 'Sorry about them,' she says, pushing down the brass lever and bringing the Plot up to steam. 'They mean well and I love them dearly, but they don't half go on.'

'It's alright,' I say. 'In a way they remind me of me and Scarlett.'

'Sisters, hey?' Emily says, putting an arm around me.

The Plot builds up to full speed and we start to cut through the water, leaving behind a broad wake that laps the side of the Bream. Without another boat out on the river, we eat up the miles and before long I catch sight of the Dry Dock jutting out from the bank.

We keep on chugging, leaving behind the brightly coloured narrow boats that are moored beside it, and continue on towards Burnham. The muddy banks of the Bream give way to a solid concrete towpath and I know we can't be far from town the moment I see the clock tower poking up over the horizon.

We pass a group of lads on the riverside, with shovels slung over their shoulders. They have a look of canal builders about them, their faces blackened with earth, and they whistle as they walk.

At the same moment the twins come and join us on the bridge. Madelyn is still only wearing a knee-length mink coat, but Evelyn is now sporting fishnet tights and suspenders, which seductively disappear into a white fur shawl that she's somehow fashioned into a dress.

'Boys ahoy!' Evelyn shouts, noticing the lads to our left.

The boys begin to run along the towpath, trying to keep up with us. Emily and I bury our heads with embarrassment. Then Madelyn brazenly opens up her coat and flashes the boys an eyeful of her naked body.

One of the lads makes a desperate leap to try and get aboard. Evelyn grabs the steering wheel and turns us away from the bank. The boy just manages to grasp some loose rope, trailing alongside the Plot; he ends up being pulled along the Bream face first.

'Scream if you want to go faster,' Evelyn says, throwing the brass lever forward.

Finally he lets go and we leave him bobbing around in the river. Evelyn and Madelyn laugh hysterically as the rest of the boys try to fish him out with their shovels.

'For God's sake!' Emily says, grabbing hold of the wheel again. 'I can't take you anywhere.'

'Come on, Emily,' I say. 'You have to admit, the look on their faces was funny.'

'Maybe,' she says, almost smiling.

'And what is it you said about that man outside the One-Eyed Monk?' I ask.

'…he'll be right as rain this time tomorrow,' we say in unison, and then we join the twins in laughter.

The twins have barely stopped giggling when the Humping Monks appear in front of us. It seems the closer we get to Burnham, the thicker the fog becomes and Emily is a little late spotting them. She has to pull really hard on the big brass lever to slow the Plot down to a halt.

'This is my stop,' I say, jumping down onto the deck and hopping ashore. 'Be careful those boys don't catch you up. Oh and watch out for those monks on your way back to the chapel too.'

'And you watch out for the man in white,' Emily says.

She and the twins wave me off as the Plot continues beneath the bridges and then disappears under the abbey wall. The moment they're gone, I head up onto street level and scan around me for any signs of Parfitt.

The mist is so thick by now, I can't even see the Angel Hotel across the other side of the square, let alone a man dressed in white. The church bells strike

121

four, making me freeze for a moment. Then I break into a run, heading down the street in the direction of home.

– The School Run of Saint Francis –

The alarm rings at precisely eight thirty, startling me
into sitting bolt upright beneath the covers. Although it
feels as if I've been smacked over the head with a
shovel during the night, I realise that if I don't show my
face in school today, they'll probably send a letter
home.

I dip my shoulders beneath the shower, dig out some
clean clothes and hurry downstairs. For once Mum
hasn't left me any breakfast, so I grab a can of Coke
and a packet of crisps from the cupboard and continue
out the back door. I try to avoid any attention as I stroll
down Saint Mary's Walks, hiding my face below my
hood.

Unlike most places that have a rush on all day,
Burnham All-Saints still has a nine o'clock rush hour
before it goes back to sleep for the rest of the day and
this morning is no different. Cars queue up at the
crossing in the central square, some of them off to
work, but most of them half-empty four-by-fours on
their way to Saint Francis.

Scarlett used to point them out to me every morning.
We would laugh at the red-faced mums struggling to
park them in the narrow lanes outside the school. But
deep down, I think they used to make her jealous. They
reminded her that no matter how hard our mum works,

people around here are generally a lot better off than we are, especially those at Saint Francis.

That's why she's so set on going to university.

I round the corner into School Lane and join the waifs and strays, that like me, still have to make the walk of shame in the morning. But as I arrive at the school gates, I realise something strange is going on.

There isn't the usual struggle for parking spaces. Instead Father Parfitt is patrolling around like a lollipop man, marshalling the cars onto the playground. A crowd has begun to swell outside the main entrance and Mrs Spraggins, the head-teacher, is standing on the steps.

I turn toward the bike sheds, where I see Jack getting off his scooter.

'Jack!' I shout, running over to him. 'What's all this about?'

'Oh, it's you,' he replies. 'Now is *really* not a good time.'

'You can't still be mad about what happened in the chapel. I just want to know what's going on.'

'No idea,' he says, lowering his voice. 'Like everybody else, I suggest you shut up and listen.'

'Fine, be like that.' I turn my back on him and push my way into the crowd. 'I don't know what Scarlett sees in you anyway.'

First bell sounds and Mrs Spraggins waits for the buzz to die down. Her hair is scraped back into a bun and held into place by a single red pencil. It's not a very flattering look, exposing her eyes that look heavily wrinkled despite being plastered beneath a thick layer of makeup.

'Now, thank you all for taking a few moments to hear what is a very important announcement,' she says. 'What I'm about to tell you will not become *news* until this evening, but with such serious ramifications I felt there was no choice but to address the school as a whole this morning.'

The hum of chitter-chatter builds up once more, as much from the parents as the students. My mind starts to wander, wondering what it could be.

'I heard that girl in Year Thirteen who's in a coma has died,' a girl next to me says to her friend. 'Gilly Thompson told me, and her mum is on the parent-governor's committee.'

'That girl is called Scarlett,' I shout angrily. 'And she's not dead, I saw her last night.'

The crowd continues to gossip, but Mrs Spraggins doesn't react. She just stands there and does what teachers always do, pausing with that look on her face. The '*how dare you speak whilst I'm speaking*' look. And after a half a minute or so, it finally quietens down enough for her to continue.

'I was deeply concerned to learn that two girls from Burnham Upper School did not return home last night.' she says, and complete silence breaks out. 'Now although they will not officially become missing

125

persons until this afternoon, the staff here at Saint Francis felt it was vital to warn you.'

'So what exactly *has* happened?' one of the mums says. 'I think we have a right to know more.'

'Are we talking abduction here?' another says. 'A serial killer?'

Mrs Spraggins raises her hand, waiting for the peace to resume. 'I'm afraid at this stage I'm unable to give you any more details. All I *am* willing to say is that school *must* continue as normal. But at the end of the school day, we will ask you all to be vigilant. Those who are being picked up by parents will be collected from the main hall and signed out. Those who are less fortunate, whose parents are not able to make it, will be escorted home. Father Parfitt has generously volunteered to organise a round robin.'

Mums indulge themselves in unreserved displays of public affection with their kids before eventually the crowd disperses, parents returning to their cars, whilst the students are marched up the steps into the school building. Everybody is lost in conversation with the person next to them, each spouting their own opinion of who did what and why.

I hang back and watch Father Parfitt as he ushers the cars out of the school gates. I'm still not entirely sure what he has to do with the ghostly goings on in the abbey the other night. But I do know that I don't trust him.

I hide behind the bike sheds and wait until all the cars have left. Then I make a run for it, realising that if I register this morning, then there's no way they'll let me go home without Mum coming to get me, or even worse, Father Parfitt walking me home.

I get as far as the market square when I decide to give Mum a call, just to let her know I'm safe. Her mobile goes straight to answerphone and I listen to her mailbox greeting. It feels strange hearing her voice; it makes me realise just how long it is since we talked – I mean, *really* talked.

'Mum, it's me, Rose,' I say, leaving her a message. 'I'm not feeling well, so I'm not going in today. I'll see you when you get home. Love you.'

As soon as I get in the back door, it's straight up to bed to catch up on my sleep. I must really need it too, because by the time I wake it's already starting to get dark.

I slump down on the sofa and take out my history coursework, turning on the television for a little bit of background noise. There's nothing much on and I barely pay attention, until the local news kicks in.

The search is on in the Suffolk town of Burnham All-Saints this afternoon. Twins, Sarah and Jessica Adams, both sixteen, were last seen leaving Burnham Upper School late on Thursday afternoon. At this stage Suffolk Police are treating the case as suspicious.

I look at their pictures. Tall, blonde, pretty…

I wonder if waking up Evelyn and Madelyn had anything to do with it. Running into the kitchen, I frantically scrawl Mum a note, telling her that I'm feeling better and that I'll see her at the hospital. Then I stomp out the back door to have it out with Emily.

I arrive at the abbey just as the church bells chime for half-past five. Dusk draws in around the ruins and I decide to slow down, knowing Emily won't rise until it gets dark.

The lights around the cathedral stretch through the thinning trees of the orchard and lead me down towards the Bream. I stroll across the wooden footbridge, noticing the Plot moored up beneath it, before heading on through the graveyard.

It's just about dark by the time I make it to the chapel and I pause awhile, staring towards the old rectory, looking out for any sign of Parfitt.

Then I pound the wooden door with my fist.

'Emily! Emily!' I shout. 'Are you there?'

There's a long pause, before I hear footsteps creeping towards me and the door slowly creaks open.

'Rose,' Emily says, still looking radiant in her green haute-neck dress. 'I wasn't expecting you until later.'

'Why?' I say, barging my way in. 'Am I interrupting something?'

'Of course not.' Emily points towards the twins, who sit in the front row painting each other's nails.

'Hi, Rose,' they say together.

'We're just getting ourselves ready for tonight. Come and join us if you want,' Madelyn says. 'You could use a little…'

'A little what?' I say.

'A spruce and shine,' Evelyn says. 'You're looking a little…'

'…shabby,' Madelyn adds.

'Well, I've got other things on my mind,' I say. 'Missing twins from Burnham Upper School. Do you know anything about it?'

'Oh, Rose,' Emily says, taking me by the arm. 'I hoped it wouldn't come to this.'

'Come to what?' I ask, pushing her away. 'What have you done?'

'Us?' the twins say.

'Nothing,' Emily says. 'But someone has.'

'If not you, then who?'

'I think you'd better sit down,' Emily says. 'It's not going to be easy for you to hear this.'

'I'll stand if it's all the same,' I say, keeping my exit clear. 'Now tell me. What sort of dark magic have you got me involved in?'

'It's not us, Rose,' Emily says, her pretty eyes open wide, pleading with me. 'I told you about the man in white, how strong he was? Well, legend has it, he's not entirely human.'

'Not human.' I say. 'Then what is he?'

'He's an immortal witch-hunter,' Emily replies.

'Immortal?' I ask, barely believing her. 'I may have agreed to help you Emily, but I thought that we were just going to wake up your sisters and then wake up mine. You didn't say anything about immortal witch-hunters.'

'I didn't really believe it myself until now. But the story goes that he draws his power from killing witches and each one he kills grants him another lifetime. You saw him yourself, sacrificing a young girl in the abbey the night after you woke me up.'

'So what are you saying? That every time we wake up one of your sisters, then he's going to take another girl from Burnham in their place?'

'Something like that,' Emily says. 'But together, we can defeat him. If we wake up the others, together we'll make a full coven of seven sisters. With your help we can open the gateway and destroy him.'

'What gateway?'

Emily points to the stone tablet beneath my feet. 'You remember the story that Jack told you, about the gateway to hell? Well… you're kind of standing on it.'

I leap backwards, my heart almost stopping in my chest. 'You said that was just a story.'

'Don't worry,' Emily says. 'You can't just fall through it. It takes a huge amount of energy to open it. But together we could. We could cast your friend the history teacher back to where he belongs and then we will put ourselves to rest on the other side. Once we're there, we'll send back Scarlett's spirit, I swear.'

I pause awhile, my thoughts swirling out of control. 'It's a lot to take in, Emily. Father Parfitt, my history teacher, some sort of supernatural witch-hunter, and us opening the gateway to hell. And what about the missing girls, what will happen to them?'

'I can't promise anything. Maybe they'll come back after he's been destroyed. But we can't do it without you, Rose. We need seven sisters.'

'Come on, Rose,' the twins say, walking up the aisle towards me. 'We need you.'

Emily stands in the middle and the three of them join hands. 'For our sisters?' she says, her eyes beckoning me over to join them.

'And what if the other girls don't come back?' I ask. 'It's just too much of a risk to take.'

'What can I say,' Emily replies. 'Nobody has ever done this before. The truth is nobody knows what will happen. Just like the doctors don't know what will happen to your sister Scarlett. That's why you need our help, in the same way that we need yours.'

Slowly I edge backwards. Every step I take, Emily takes one too.

'I'm sorry, Emily,' I say, pulling open the door behind me. 'I'll have to let you know on this one. But right now I've got to see Scarlett.'

I run up the shingle path and through the entire estate without a single glance over my shoulder. Thankfully the abbey gates are still open as I make it into the market square. Hurrying across town, I try to

131

put Emily and what she said about Father Parfitt to the back of my mind, focusing my thoughts on beating Mum to the hospital.

The waiting room is full when I arrive – not that I'm surprised, as it's always busy on a Friday evening. I glance up at the silver clock on the wall; it's only half-past six, which means that visiting hours won't start for another half an hour. Then I pull my hood up over my head and carry on up the main corridor regardless.

I pass the reception desk at Intensive Care; the woman who works there is lost in her crossword magazine, so I continue onto the ward. All is quiet, there are no doctors, no nurses, and I can even hear the machine keeping Scarlett alive.

But when I turn the corner, suddenly I stop.

Father Parfitt stands there, leaning over Scarlett's lifeless body, a leather bible in one hand and a candle in the other. I wonder why he's there, what his intentions are. Our eyes meet. I try to speak, but words won't come.

Then a shot of adrenaline pulses through my body and instincts take over.

– Nowhere to Run –

I turn around and run out of Scarlett's ward, desperately searching for Mum. Slowing down at the reception desk, I hesitate for a moment, waiting to see if Father Parfitt will follow. The receptionist looks over the top of her magazine and stares right at me, a puzzled look etched across her face.

'My sister is in terrible danger,' I say. 'I think she might be…'

'In a state of distress?' the receptionist asks, chewing on her pen lid. 'Five letters, begins with a P.'

'Don't worry,' I say. 'You wouldn't understand.'

I weave through the crowded main corridor, like a fish swimming against the stream. My hurried footsteps are masked by a pelting noise striking the flat roof above me.

It's not until I reach the car park that I realise what the noise was. A cloud has burst in the sky and a fierce wind spits its full force into my face. My eyes narrow, hoping to catch sight of Bluebell's battered paintwork amongst the endless rows of shiny new cars.

People hurry out of their vehicles towards the main entrance, grimacing against the storm. Then I notice a man in a long camel overcoat, lingering at the parking machine. One of his hands rifles through his pockets, desperately seeking the correct change, whilst the other

133

clings to a newspaper that he's using to shield his head from the rain.

'Excuse me,' I say, pulling at his sleeve. 'My sister is in danger. I need your help.'

He lowers the newspaper to reveal his face. He's of African descent, his dark skin speckled with age beneath a mass of tight greying curls. Then I see the white clerical collar gleaming around his neck – and the same crucifix worn by Father Parfitt.

'Sorry,' I say. 'I thought you were someone else.'

Stepping out into the centre of the car park, I stand beneath the pouring rain, letting it soak me to the skin.

'Mum, where are you?' I scream.

Then for some reason that I can't explain, I suddenly get an urge to run. With no idea where I'm going, I sprint straight out of the car park and into the road. I pass the shopping centre on Auction Rise and continue into the market square.

I don't know whether it's the fear of a serial killer on the loose or the torrential rain, but as the wind sears against my cheeks, there's not a single person in sight.

Eventually I stop, right in the middle of the Humping Monks, and I climb up onto the wall. I stand there looking down at the Bream, raindrops striking its surface, casting giant circles. Then I stretch out my arms like a crucifix and close my eyes.

'Somebody, help me!' I shout. 'Please…'

The next thing I know, my eyes slowly open and I'm lying out on the deck of the Plot. Emily is holding a bottle beneath my nose, whilst the twins kneel a few paces behind her. I take a swig from the bottle and the rancid taste of tree-sap vodka hits the back of my throat, waking me up with a start.

'How did I get here?' I say.

'Rose, you fell from the bridge,' Emily says. 'We pulled you from the water.'

'How did you know I was there?'

'Sisters know when each other are in danger. Like it or not, you're one of us now.'

'That's right, Rose,' the twins say. 'We're bound together.'

'What about Father Parfitt?'

'What about him?' Emily replies.

'I saw him at Scarlett's bedside,' I say. 'What if he's turned off her life-support machine and stolen her soul.'

'He wouldn't. Trust me, if he is the man in white, then it's not his style. He's more of a showman than that.'

'I've got to go,' I say, trying to get onto my feet. 'I've got to stop him.'

'And *we* will stop him, Rose,' Emily says. 'But we'll need you at full strength first. In fact, we'll need a full coven of seven sisters at full strength to stop him.'

The three of them drag me below deck and lay me out on one of the long wooden benches by the fire. The warmth brings back my senses and I feel the weight of my wet clothes stuck to my skin. Emily goes to the cupboard and pulls out a black velvet cat-suit. Then the

135

twins appear behind her, holding a sleeveless fur body-warmer with a long droopy hood.

'We made these for you,' Emily says. 'So you can look like one of us, but still look like yourself.'

'Come on,' Madelyn says. 'You must be freezing.'

Slowly I stand up and together they help pull the heavy clothes from my back. I rest my weight on Emily's shoulder as I step into the cat-suit, and for a moment, I feel exposed. The twins' hands stray all over my naked body, stretching the velvet up over my shoulders.

'It fits perfectly,' Emily says, fastening me up at the front.

'And now for the coat,' Evelyn says excitedly.

The second I slip it on I feel revitalised. The soft lining of the hood strokes my cheeks, warming my scalp beneath my wet hair. Emily thrusts a bottle into my hand and I knock it back. With tree-sap vodka coursing through my veins, suddenly I feel invincible.

'Let's do this,' I say. 'Let's take him down.'

– Stand and Deliver –

The crackle of hot coals competes with the patter of rain, as the four of us gather below deck of the Plot. Emily and I sit shoulder to shoulder, staring across at the twins who are still dressed like a couple of cheap tarts, their hair now tied up in pigtails, fastened with brightly coloured ribbons that match their painted toenails.

'So which sister should we wake up next?' I ask.

'Well, Hope is by far the closest.' Emily says, getting up and walking towards the stove. 'He killed her in the abbey itself.'

'But she'll be the hardest,' the twins say. 'The place is crawling with monks.'

'So best we leave her to last,' I say. 'When we're up to full strength.'

'Agreed,' Emily says, picking up a long piece of metal that's sat next to the stove. 'That leaves Paige or Alice.'

'Who was killed first?' I ask.

'Alice.' Emily stabs the poker into the embers of the fire, making it roar. 'He pressed her to death under the heavy stones of Grim's Graves.'

'Grim's Graves?' I say. 'That'll be quite a trek. It's twenty miles away, right up on the other side of the county border.'

'That's the one.' Emily removes the poker, which is now red-hot, and sticks it into a brass bucket of water, making it sizzle. 'We'll take the Plot as far as the Dry Dock. Then we'll rustle up some horses and cut across land. With a bit of luck we'll be there and back before sunrise.'

'So what are we waiting for?' I say.

'Twins,' orders Emily. 'Get up on deck. It's your turn to drive.'

'Do we have to? It's cold and wet up there and it'll make our hair go frizzy.'

'Well, if you don't go, it'll make your hair go shorter,' Emily says. 'Because I'll take those pigtails and pull them off the side of your scalps with my bare hands.'

The twins disappear up the ladder and onto the bridge, slamming the hatch closed behind them.

'Now we can actually hear ourselves think, I need you to read Alice's page,' Emily says, pulling her beloved book from a drawer beneath my seat. 'You need to know exactly what you are getting yourself into. You need to know who we're up against.'

I take the heavy book into my hand. Although I rested my palm on it the night we woke up the twins, it's the first time I've actually held it since we broke into the museum – since I realised what it was made from.

I pull open the thick leather cover and flick through the first few pages. They're a mouldy brown colour and the handwritten text is almost illegible. All I can really make out is the title, *The Act of Witchcraft,* and the date, *1602.*

I carry on reading, skimming over a few sketches of what can only be described as torture devices, until I come to a break. Several leafs have been torn from the spine, leaving little jagged edges like teeth. Then all of a sudden the texture changes, almost as if the pages have been laminated, and I see the name *Alice Manley* at the top.

I run my finger below the words, trying to read them. The very thought that I'm touching human skin sends a shiver up my spine.

'Alice Manley, a gravedigger at Burnham All-Saints Chapel, tried in accordance with the Act of Witchcraft on May 2nd 1692,' I read.

'Go on,' Emily says, turning her back to me and pacing back towards the stove.

'The accused was first suspected of bringing the devil amongst the good people of Burnham All-Saints when she was captured coming to the aid of known witches on the eve of May 1st 1692. After spending the night in the Clock Tower Jail, she was taken to Grim's Graves on the morning of May 2nd 1692.'

The text becomes smudged and the decorative font difficult to read, so Emily comes and sits beside me to help.

'The accused was then encouraged to confess, by method of pressing,' she says. 'Ten hours and three stones later, she was pronounced dead. As the good Lord would not allow innocence to suffer such pain, it can only be concluded that Alice Manley was indeed guilty of witchcraft.'

'What's pressing?' I ask.

'It was horrific,' Emily says. 'Giant slabs of bedrock, so heavy three men had to hoist them up on pulleys. Then slowly they were lowered onto Alice's body, as she lay bound to an altar. The first one crushed her legs, the next her stomach, and the last one her head.'

'Where were you? Did you see it happen?'

'We were there,' Emily says, tears now streaming down her face. 'Me, Hope and Paige. He shackled us together and made us watch. He said he'd spare her if we all confessed. But Alice told us not to.'

'She must have been really brave,' I say.

'Not only that,' Emily says, wiping her cheeks and laughing a little. 'She's fairly stupid too.'

'It's okay, Emily,' I say. 'We'll have her back before sunrise.'

'I hope you're right. This one is going to be much more dangerous than waking the twins. You do know why he chose to kill her at Grim's Graves, don't you?'

'Because she was a gravedigger? You said it yourself. He was a bit of a showman.'

'I'm sure that had something to do with it,' Emily says. 'But what do you actually know about Grim's Graves?'

140

'Not a lot. As far as I know they date back to the Stone Age. They're mineshafts dug out by the druids to find flint for tools. I think they even tried to mine coal from them in more recent times.'

'That might be true. But it was the Anglo Saxons who named them. They called them Grim's Graves after one of their gods. He was a dark hooded man, with a big iron pickaxe and a pack of wild dogs. He was God of the Hunt or something.'

'He sounds a bit like the Grim Reaper,' I say. 'I wonder if he's any relation.'

'Why don't you ask, when you see him?' Emily rolls her eyes upward. 'But seriously, the twins and I might be in more danger than you with this one.'

'I don't understand. You're already dead – what can harm you?'

'As the God of the Hunt, it was Grim's job to clear away the dead,' Emily says. 'They say he still haunts the mines, dragging lost souls down to the underworld and making them work there for the rest of eternity.'

'He won't be a match for the four of us. Surely?'

'I don't know. But it's better to be ready.' Emily pulls open a drawer beneath the bench opposite us. 'I've kept hold of Ned's shotgun just in case. I want you to take it.'

'Why me? Why don't you have it?'

'Because you're still alive, Rose. He can't drag your soul away,' Emily says. 'I need you to watch over the rest of us. Can you do it?'

141

'Of course,' I say, standing up and strapping the gun across my back. 'Sisters have got to stick together.'

'But be careful. Don't shoot unless it's really necessary. It's only got one load left in it.'

The rain has died down to a light drizzle by the time we step onto the bridge, but it's left its mark on the Bream; it's swollen banks are bursting at the edges. The Dry Dock appears on the horizon, so Emily takes the wheel, carefully guiding the bow beneath the boatshed. Then she sends the twins down to moor us up.

'Take a look around for anything useful,' Emily says, packing her leather satchel with her book. 'We've got a fair few miles ahead of us.'

'Hair done,' Evelyn says.

'Nails done,' Madelyn adds.

'Please!' Emily scowls. 'Can you two think of something other than the way you look for a single moment?'

'What about this?' I say, picking up a small metal anchor tied to a length of rope. 'It might come in handy if we're going down mineshafts.'

'Good work,' Emily says. 'Anything else?'

'What about these?' the twins say, pointing out two planks of wood. 'We can use them to keep our feet dry.'

'There's no way I'm ruining this pedicure,' Madelyn adds. 'Not even for Alice.'

We step out onto the towpath, climbing a steep bank into a field of cropped straw. The twins' deck boards come in really handy and we lay them down one at a time, using them as stepping stones to cross the waterlogged soil. But it's slow progress and it takes nearly half an hour before we pick up anything that could be described as a road.

'We'll never make it at this rate,' I say.

'Don't worry, now we're on the path we can steal ourselves some horses,' Emily says. 'Rose, have you ever been stagecoach robbing before?'

'It's not something they teach you at school,' I say. 'But I do know that you're supposed to shout *stand and deliver* at the end.'

'Well, there's a little more to it than that,' Emily says, laughing. 'It requires two things.'

'Speed,' Evelyn says excitedly.

'And surprise,' Madelyn adds. 'I do love a good hold-up.'

We follow the path for a mile or more as it crests a gentle rise and then dips into a valley. A large moon rises through the clouds and although it's not quite full, I get the feeling that this time tomorrow, it will be. It illuminates the path like a giant floodlight, making our task of hiding almost impossible.

A few metres more and we pass a blind bend, lined by a grove of evergreen pine trees. 'This is the spot,' Emily says, her pretty eyes darting from side to side, weighing up our chances. 'All we need now is something to make them stop.'

'I've got that covered,' Madelyn says, undoing the top button of her mink coat.

'Sister, I like your way of thinking,' Emily says. 'Rose, you come off the road and help me with the surprise part.'

'And what should I do?' asks Evelyn.

'I don't know. What can you do?' Emily sighs. 'Look after my satchel and the book. Oh, and help your twin sister with the distraction too.'

I give Emily a boost as she shimmies up one of the pine trees. Then I sling the rope up to her and she lodges the anchor around a sturdy-looking branch. I'm just looking for a suitable foothold so I can join her, when she cuts in and breaks my concentration.

'No, you stay down low,' she says. 'When they come to a halt, I'll swing down and hit them from the side. Then you walk out slowly and hold the gun up in front of them. Don't say too much and don't fire, not unless it gets ugly. Remember there's only one bullet.'

'Understood,' I say.

The wind whistles through the trees and we wait for what seems like an eternity. Then finally the rattle of cartwheels bouncing across rough terrain comes rumbling over the horizon. Four chestnut horses follow, tethered to a single-axle trailer. Two men perch on an open bench at the front, reins held firmly in their hands. Behind them is an oblong-shaped carriage, with clear glass windows almost as big as doors.

'Whoa there,' one of the drivers says, spotting the twins out in the road. 'What have we got here?'

'Just a couple of girls lost in the cold,' Madelyn says, undoing the rest of the buttons of her coat and letting it fall open seductively.

The man nearest to us steps down and walks towards her. He's wearing knee-high leather boots that disappear into a long black trench coat. Even from a distance, it's clear to see that he's tall and powerfully built, with long blond hair flowing freely around his shoulders.

'How did a couple of pretty things like you end up out here then?' he says, gently running one of Madelyn's pigtails against his cheek and then giving it a sniff. 'What happened to your horses?'

At that moment Emily swoops down from the trees and kicks the other man clear off his perch, knocking him out cold. She lets go of the rope as it swings back and lands perfectly balanced in the middle of the carriage.

'Stand and deliver!' she shouts. 'Or I'll run you down in your boots, right where you're standing.'

The big blond man turns and begins to laugh loudly. At the same moment one of the horses bolts, kicking out at the carriage. Emily is thrown off balance and falls headfirst from the side. She tries to grasp hold of the reins on the way down, but doesn't quite manage it and ends up tangled beneath the wheels.

The blond man grabs the twins by the pigtails and drags them down on the floor. 'I guessed it was a little too good to be true,' he says. 'But there's no way we're getting turned over by a pack of girls.'

'Is that right?' I say, gathering myself together and coming out of the brush with Ned's shotgun pointed at his head.

'Now, now, my dear,' he says, undoing his coat to reveal a white dog-collar. 'I'm sure you wouldn't shoot a man of the cloth.'

'Don't tempt me,' I say, holding my ground. 'Take one step closer and I'll blow a hole in your head so big, your whole fist will fit through it.'

'I don't think you will,' he says, edging ever closer. 'I don't think you've got the...'

'Balls?' I say, my finger poised over the trigger.

He makes a sudden run towards me, his arms reaching out at my gun. I shut my eyes and squeeze the trigger. There's a loud bang. The butt of the rifle recoils into my shoulder and twists me around sideways.

I turn back to see that my bullet has hit him just above his right eye. Half his head is missing; blood oozes out of his shattered skull and leaks onto his shoulder. He continues to walk towards me. His fingers tighten around the barrels of my shotgun, ripping it from my hands. Then he crumples in a heap onto the ground.

There's a long silence.

'Everyone alright?' I say, my heart still racing.

'We're good,' the twins say, scurrying to their feet.

'Emily?' I say.

'I'm alright, I just got the wind knocked out of me,' she says, jumping back onto the carriage. 'Check their pockets for anything useful and let's get out of here.'

The twins rush over to the man lying by the carriage, whilst I see to his friend. I kick at his corpse, so that he's spread out on his back, his fingers still tightly gripped around both barrels of my shotgun. I look at what's left of his face and at the blood-splattered dog collar around his neck. Then I take in a deep breath and rummage through his pockets.

'Nothing but a bible on this one,' I say.

'Nothing here either,' the twins say.

'Come on then,' Emily says, taking her satchel back from Evelyn. 'Let's go.'

Nobody says a word as we pull away, not even the twins. The roar of hooves pounding the road booms ahead of us, and the rattle of wheels clattering over broken stones echoes behind. Emily grips the reins tightly, despite wincing every time we go over a bump. And although she won't admit it, I get the feeling she's must have fallen harder than she's let on.

'Why don't you let the twins drive?' I say. 'You could have a lie-down in the back.'

'I don't mind letting them drive,' Emily says. 'But there's no way I'm lying down back there.'

I turn around and take a look through the glass doors of the carriage. There's a wooden coffin with shiny brass handles, sitting there, on a red velvet blanket.

'No way,' I say, shaking my head. 'I don't believe it.'

'What do you mean?' Emily says, handing the reins onto the twins and opening up the carriage doors.

'Well, coffins aren't usually carried around on scruffy old carts with rusty wheels,' I say. 'And the man I shot, he didn't talk like a preacher man.'

'Preacher men don't wear their hair like that either,' Emily says, nodding. 'Are you thinking what I'm thinking?'

We rush into the back and kneel either side of the closed casket. Emily clutches at her ribs with one hand, flicking open the latches with the other. Then she slowly lifts the lid and pushes it towards me.

'Well, well, well,' she says, smiling. 'What have we got here?'

I look down to see a bunch of open books with false compartments instead of pages, a pistol-shaped crossbow with an ivory handle, a quiver full of arrows and fifteen glass bottles labelled up as moonshine.

'Bootleggers,' I say. 'Or smugglers?'

'Who cares,' Emily says. 'You take the bow. And I'll put a couple of these bottles in my bag for later. I get a feeling we'll need a drink before the night is out.'

We go back and sit up front, on either side of the twins. The horses drop their heads and push on through

148

as the path begins to wind its way through woodland. Having just been on the other end of an ambush, I realise that we're in a vulnerable position. So I load up the crossbow and rest it across my forearm, ready to fire at anything that moves.

'With all the panic, I forgot to say thanks,' Emily says, taking a crafty swig from one of the bottles to ease her pain. 'You did good back there.'

'Don't worry about it,' I say, my eyes scanning the bushes. 'I was just looking out for my sisters, like you told me to.'

– Alice –

The tall evergreen pines begin to thin out as the path bends around chopped down tree-stumps and mounds of slag. The ground by the wayside looks scarred, pockmarked with discarded flint-stone from years of mining. At the top of a slight hill is a huge stone monolith, bathed in moonlight, looking like a plinth to those who toiled beneath it. And just below, there's the entrance to a tunnel.

'Looks like we're here,' Emily says. 'Twins, I want you to stay up here and tend to the horses, while Rose and I go in and get Alice.'

'Do we have to?' the twins whine. 'What about Grim?'

'If he's real, then he's down there in the tunnel,' Emily says. 'You'll be safer here.'

'And a lot less trouble,' I add quietly.

I catch Emily smile as she takes one of the glass bottles from her satchel and stuffs the neck full of dry leaves. 'Here, Rose,' she says. 'Give me a hand with this.'

We sit down cross-legged, with our fingers entwined and the bottle between us. 'I channel the Earth in the name of my sisters,' Emily says. 'Air, soil, water and fire.'

We repeat it together, over and over.

'Aeternus Ignis!' Emily says, sharply raising her voice along with our hands.

The leaves in the top of the bottle begin to smoulder and a little flame licks its way over the rim. 'That should do it,' Emily says, standing up and slinging her satchel across her back. 'Are you ready?'

I cock my crossbow, making a loud crunching noise. 'Ready as I'll ever be.'

We step beneath a thick stone collar and into the barrel of the mine. Emily's torchlight carries a few metres ahead, illuminating the sharp jagged edges of the axe-ravaged walls. We're only a few steps in when there's a howl from above. We both stop dead and turn to look at each other.

'What was that?' I ask. 'It sounded like a hunting dog.'

'Probably just an owl or something,' Emily says. 'Come on, let's get this over with, before it wakes up Grim.'

We wade deeper inside, the timber beams groaning under the weight of the earth above us. A maze of tight corridors branch off from the main shaft in all directions, but Emily continues straight on, as if she knows exactly where she's going.

Skeletons line the way, their white bones coated in cinder shard. Many of them stand as if they're working and some even have tools still grasped between their fingers. But nothing stops Emily. The light from of her torch strokes her face and I see her bright green eyes, barely blinking, focused forward.

Eventually we burst into a broad hollow. Stalactites hang from the ceiling and a circle of large rounded stones sit around an altar in the centre.

'This is it,' Emily says, finding a flat surface to sit on and opening her satchel. 'This is where he did it.'

She opens her book face down on the rough terrain and we both place our palms on the cover. 'I channel the Earth in the name of my sisters,' we say together, using exactly the same words at the same time. 'Air, soil, water and fire.'

'Sorores in Aeternum!' Emily screams, her voice echoing off the walls of the cave.

The naked body of a woman appears laid out on the altar. Slowly she stands up, casting a long shadow that stretches halfway up the walls behind her. Then she starts striding towards us. The closer she gets, the bigger she looks. Her hair is wild, spiked on top with long rattails running down her back. She's got broad shoulders like a man and a thick, jutting jaw. By the time she's standing over us, I realise she must be over six feet tall.

'Alice,' Emily says. 'This is Rose, your new sister. The twins are outside. We're here to rescue you.'

'Alice not understand,' she says in broken English. 'Alice doesn't need rescuing.'

'We'll explain later,' Emily says slowly. 'But right now, we've got to get going.'

'Alice want to dig,' she says, stamping her feet. 'Alice not going anywhere.'

'I think I saw a shovel in the hand of one of the skeletons,' I say, pointing to the mineshaft behind us. 'Come on, let's go.'

'There you go,' Emily says. 'Alice, come now and dig later.'

We run up the main corridor. Emily leads the way whilst I lag behind with Alice who has to stoop below the roof trusses. Together we kick at the bones of the dead miners, desperately trying to find a spade. We're almost at the top when we eventually get lucky and find one. Alice lets out a childlike roar of excitement. It booms the entire length of the mineshaft and almost starts a landslide.

'Steady on,' Emily says. 'We don't want to wake up Grim.'

'Who is Grim?' Alice says.

'Don't worry,' Emily says angrily. 'Just come on for heaven's sake!'

We burst outside into the night. Stood below the moon and a sky full of twinkling stars, it almost seems like daytime. I spot the twins up ahead – they're already sitting in the driving seat of the carriage, reins in hand and ready to go.

Then a large bird swoops from the sky and lands on Alice's shovel. 'Alice found a birdy,' she says, gently turning her neck, trying not to disturb it.

The bird walks down the shaft of her spade and sits on her shoulder.

'Would you look at that,' Emily says.

Even on Alice's giant sloping shoulders, the bird is big. It has brown dappled feathers, thick yellow feet and a hook-shaped beak that looks as sharp as a hunting knife.

'I think it's a bird of prey,' I say. 'A buzzard or something.'

A whistling noise comes from above. The bird takes off, circling in the sky before sweeping behind the large rock on top of the mineshaft. Then a hooded figure appears, with a large pickaxe in one hand and the bird sitting obediently in the other.

'Who is that?' Alice asks innocently.

'That's Grim,' Emily says, pulling open the doors of the carriage. 'I told you not to wake him!'

Alice clambers into the carriage first and sits on top of the coffin, still without a stitch of clothing on. Emily scurries up one side and I squeeze down on the other, my crossbow aimed and ready. Then the twins crack the reins and the horses break into a canter.

The buzzard flutters around the sky, diving down and taking pot-shots at us. It makes the horses a little skittish and the cart begins to rattle worse than ever.

There's a loud howl, like the one we heard earlier. A set of eyes appears, glowing at the mouth of the mineshaft. First one pair, then two, but before long there are too many to count.

Blue-eyed wolf dogs pour out of the tunnel, their light-coloured fur painted silver by the moon. They soon make up the ground between us, barking loudly, showing off their sharp, angry teeth.

I steady my crossbow as the carriage jolts over the bumpy road. Then I let rip, hitting one straight in the sternum. His front legs splay to the sides. His chin strikes the ground and he lets out a sad whimper.

Emily joins me at the back of the carriage, throwing the bottle she's been using as a torch. It hits the dog closest to us and he bursts into flames, still running along behind for a few strides before he tumbles into a ball of fire.

'I haven't got enough arrows to shoot them all down,' I gasp. 'And we'll never outrun them.'

'It's alright, I've got an idea,' Emily says. 'Alice, can you stand up?'

'Alice stand,' she replies, crouching above the coffin with her head pushed against the carriage's roof.

'Right, Rose,' Emily says. 'Grab the other side and get ready to push.'

We slide the casket across the velvet blanket so that it's hanging out the back of the carriage. Two dogs close in on us, spit dripping off their tongues as they growl below our feet.

'Right Alice, sit down and kick!' Emily urges.

Alice does as she's told, dropping her bum down behind the coffin and launching it out the back of the carriage with her giant feet. It hits the two chasing dogs square on and then shatters across the road. Debris sprays out the sides and the remaining bottles inside smash, taking out a couple more dogs.

'They're still coming,' I say to Emily. 'And they're gaining on us.'

'We'll have to shed more weight.' Emily opens the doors behind Alice. 'Come on!'

'Alice cold,' she says, rising to her feet and following Emily up front.

'Here, take this,' I say.

I pick up the red velvet blanket from the floor and tie it around Alice's neck. Then I poke my head through the carriage door to listen to Emily's plan.

'Right, twins,' Emily says, grabbing the reins. 'I need you to get on those horses at the front.'

'Slow down and we will,' Madelyn says.

'We can't!' Emily points at a wolf dog that's made it right alongside the horses. 'There's not time.'

I take an arrow from my quiver and load up. Then I nail him straight through the hindquarters and he pulls up lame. 'I can't hold them off much longer,' I shout, noticing two more pulling out from under our wheels.

'Now!' Emily says.

The twins take a step back onto the bench and then leap towards the first row of horses. They land together, perfectly synchronised, each with a saddle straddled between their thighs. Grabbing handfuls of mane, they climb up their horses' necks and then dive forward, clambering onto the next row of horses at the front.

156

'Good work!' Emily says. 'Now, Rose, you help Alice onto one.'

'Alice can't,' she says.

'Alice can,' I say, lining her up behind the nearest horse on the left. 'On three.'

Alice leans forward, her legs bent at ninety, like she's about to dive into a swimming pool. 'One, two, three,' I say, and then push her over the edge.

She falls face first onto the horse's back, her red cape billowing behind, baring the cheeks of her bum. Then her legs fall either side of the saddle and she sits up straight.

'Now for you, Rose,' Emily says. 'And don't hang around, we've got company.'

I turn around to see a wolf in the carriage behind. I load up and shoot him straight between the eyes. Then I kick the carriage door shut.

'What about you?' I say. 'There's only one horse left.'

'I'm going to wind up riding with you,' Emily says. 'Leave me your middle stirrup.'

I wedge my crossbow behind my quiver and then take the same approach as the twins, using the bench seat as leverage. I take a running jump into the air. But I overshoot. My arms end up wrapped around the horse's neck, my inside leg slung across his back and the other leg dangling down towards the ground.

I kick out my trailing leg until my foot finds the outside stirrup. Then I pull myself up.

'Emily, hurry,' I cry, glancing back to see the carriage now filled with dogs.

Emily places her hands on the hindquarters of the first two horses. Then she swings herself forward so that her left foot is in Alice's middle stirrup and her right foot is in mine.

Standing up straight, she takes an arrow from my quiver and then bends forward. With her head between her own legs, she goes to work on the leather straps.

'When we break off, try and keep as close to Alice as you can,' she says, coming up for air.

Then she bends back down and finishes the job.

The horses break free. The carriage flips up on its single axle and catapults the dogs into the air. Emily stands up straight, still with one foot in my stirrup and one in Alice's. She kicks her left foot clear. Then she swings her weight around, so she's sitting behind me, facing backwards with her spine pushed against mine.

She takes the bow from my back, loads it up and shoots the chasing buzzard that is right above my head. Then she slaps our horse hard across its rump and we disappear into the night.

We work the horses hard, keeping them at a gallop the whole length of the road. We don't even rest them to cross the muddy field that leads back to the towpath, making them hack through it, almost up to their knees.

By the time we reach the Dry Dock, the horses' tongues are drooping out of their mouths and their heads are hanging to the side. We lead them slowly in

158

through the stable doors, where the Plot is moored up waiting.

'Take your horses to water, it's the least they deserve,' Emily says. 'And then pat them goodbye.'

We all do as she says before making our way up onto the Plot. Emily is last to step aboard, still clutching at her bruised ribs. Then she opens up her satchel and hands a bottle of moonshine to each of us.

'Right, now it's our turn to drink!' she says.

The twins remain at the helm, steering us out onto the Bream. But the rest of us disappear below deck to drink to our sisters and lick our wounds. The air inside is stale from the fire and before long I feel myself getting drowsy.

At some point I doze off, until morning comes slashing through the portholes and stirs me. I look outside to see that we're just beneath the Humping Monks and the sun is rising above the abbey walls. The Plot gently comes to a halt as I make my way on deck Then slowly I get myself together and say goodbye to the girls.

– Dead Letter –

The church bells chime seven as I make my way up the steps towards street level. I'm surprised to see the central square so empty. By this time of day, the market traders would usually be out in hats and gloves, setting up their stalls for the Saturday morning rush.

But instead, it's just me and the pigeons.

I begin to wonder what's going on, until my mind turns to more urgent matters. Mum must have hit the roof when she didn't find me at the hospital yesterday evening and the fact that I didn't come home later must have sent her over the edge. Especially with the rumour of a killer on the loose, she's probably called the police.

I resist the temptation of cutting through Saint Mary's Walks and take the long way around, wondering whether I'll see any police cars waiting out the front. Much to my surprise, the scene looks amazingly quiet: no drama, just Bluebell parked at the kerb a few metres from our door.

I turn the key and step into the hallway. 'Mum, it's only me,' I say. 'I'm home.'

I wait a moment, but nothing happens.

I wait some more.

Still nothing.

I continue down the corridor to the kitchen. The place looks a mess. Dirty dishes piled up in the sink, clothes hanging out of the washing machine and muddy footprints all over the floor. Then I see two pieces of paper on the kitchen table. One is the handwritten note I left for Mum last night, but the other is more formal-looking, typed up on headed paper.

I pick it up and start reading.

Dear Mrs Glover,

I am writing to you regarding our meeting on Thursday 29th October. Having observed your daughter since her accident, I have to conclude that all brain activity ceased over two weeks ago. After a difficult conversation, we both agreed that life-support should be terminated. As we discussed, this will take place at 9.00 A.M. on Sunday, November 1st.

I confirm that I will be in attendance, along with our grief counselling service. I have also arranged for the attendance of Father Parfitt, in accordance to your wishes. Please do not hesitate to contact me in the interim, should you feel the need of my assistance.

Yours regretfully,
Doctor Brown

The words take a moment to register. Then suddenly I can't breathe. It's like somebody just pulled my heart out from my chest and stamped on it in front of me.

'Mum!' I shout. 'Mum, what's this letter all about?'

I stomp up the stairs and look around the landing. Steam curls beneath the bathroom door and the sound of running water echoes around the upper floor. I turn the handle, but the blasted thing is locked, so I start to beat on it with my fist.

'Mum, let me in!' I shout. 'We need to talk.'

There's no reply.

I take three steps back. Then I drop my shoulder and charge. The lock breaks through the flimsy wooden frame and the door bursts open. Mum's sitting there on the toilet, fully clothed, her head buried in her hands. The taps are running in the bath and water is flowing over the side and soaking the rug.

I turn off the taps and walk over towards Mum, waving the letter in her face. 'What's this?'

'The letter.' Mum raises her head up from her hands. 'It's the letter.'

'And when were you going to tell me?'

'She left me a letter,' she says, her eyes avoiding mine. 'It said she was feeling better.'

'Mum, I left you that letter. I'm talking about this letter. The one from the doctor about you killing Scarlett.'

'She's going to die,' Mum says, bursting into tears. 'My little girl is going to die.'

'She doesn't have to, Mum,' I say. 'Give it another week. She'll wake up, I promise. I can't tell you how, but I know she will, just trust me.'

But Mum doesn't seem to take any notice. She just rocks back and forwards. The colour has drained from her skin, and her eyes are darting around the room.

'Only just eighteen and her whole life ahead of her,' she says. 'My precious little daughter.'

'I'm never going to forgive you for this,' I say, throwing the letter onto the wet floor and storming down the stairs.

I make it as far as the kitchen until it all becomes too much. It's as if the walls are closing in on me. Every room filled with memories of Scarlett, the photos in the hallway, her clothes hanging out of the washing machine. So I open the back door to get some air and without a thought I just keep walking.

I stagger out of Saint Mary's Walks and continue towards the central square. Traffic speeds past me as the world goes about their business. But it all seems a bit of a blur.

Mum and I have both been under a lot of stress over the past few weeks. But reading that letter, looking at Mum, just an empty shell about to lie down and let Father Parfitt murder my sister – it's like the bottom just fell out of my world.

I'm right in the middle of the square when I finally come back to my senses. I realise the market still hasn't started. Instead of haggling over their fresh fruit and veg, the good people of Burnham All-Saints have all come together. There's far too many of them to count: more than a hundred, maybe even a thousand. They're each holding a candle and walking beneath the open portcullis of the Norman Tower in a long orderly line.

For a moment, I wonder if I'm dreaming.

163

Maybe they've all heard about Scarlett and come to pay their final respects?

But then again, why would they?

It's not as if she's that important to anyone around here, only me.

Muscling my way in, I join the queue and follow them into the abbey. It's not until I make my way to the front that everything becomes clear. Leading the line, both dressed in white, are Father Parfitt and the African priest that I saw outside the hospital yesterday.

They continue up the steps of the cathedral and in through the giant oak doors. They're first to lay their candles in the chancel. Then a full-strength choir bursts into song. I sit in the middle somewhere, watching as others follow, placing down their candles and taking their seats. Before long, Parfitt and his new friend can barely move around the parapet, as the floor is covered in a golden blanket of light.

The choir continues to sing until every pew is taken and the room falls silent.

'Good people of Burnham All-Saints,' Father Parfitt says, holding up his hands as he addresses the crowd. 'As I look out at the faces before me, a single thought comes to my mind. That on this morning, as the people of this town send an overwhelming message of support, there are three faces missing.'

'Did he say three?' I say, turning to the woman next to me.

'Shh!' she replies, holding her finger up to her lips.

164

'When my phone rang this morning, to tell me that another young woman had failed to return home, I knew something had to be done,' Father Parfitt continues. 'And even though it fills my heart with much sadness, the way in which you have responded at least fills me with some hope. Let us pray.'

He bursts into the Lord's Prayer and the congregation bow their heads. My eyes dart around, unable to look Father Parfitt. His words seem so hollow.

I stare up at the huge stone pillars that lead towards the vaulted ceiling. I wonder how he can stand there and spout such lies, in a cathedral of all places, in the house of God.

There's a long pause while people reflect. Then Parfitt has the cheek to start up again. 'In these sad circumstances, it gives me some comfort to introduce you all to an old friend of mine. The newly ordained Archbishop of East Anglia. Ladies and gentlemen, I give you the Reverend John Mensah.'

'Thanks, Father Parfitt,' says the Archbishop, picking up a candle from the floor. 'In these difficult times, I try to remind myself that life is like a light. A candle that cannot burn forever.'

The Archbishop purses his thick brown lips and gently blows out the candle. He waits awhile as a tiny train of smoke rises and disappears into the vast tower above him.

'Whether it's cruelly blown out before its time, or whether it simply burns itself out, at some point the candle's flame must go out,' he says. 'But the light that it has given us along the way, now, that is eternal. That is the eternal love of the Holy Father.'

The gleaming light of the candles beneath his feet spreads around the room, warming the faces of the congregation. Their cheeks glisten. Tears begin to flow. By the time the choir starts up again, there's not a dry eye in the house.

Several prayers and some forty minutes later, the good people of Burnham start to leave, in a long orderly line, just as they arrived. I pull my hood up to cover my face and bow down in my seat, listening to Father Parfitt and the Archbishop as they stand by the doors, offering some final words of comfort to the grieving masses.

Then the door booms shut. The pair walk back up the aisle and disappear through a side door in the transept. I get the urge to follow, desperate to know what they're really saying and whether Father Parfitt's new friend is in on it.

I creep behind them, three or four paces behind as we enter one of the side chapels. It's little more than a long corridor; big stained glass windows run along one side, soaking the stone floor in light, making it look like a brightly coloured mosaic. The other side is bolted to the cathedral with thick-necked buttresses, which are perfect to hide behind as I track the pair towards the vestry.

They disappear inside and close the door behind them, so I push my ear to its rough surface and listen to their conversation.

'Thanks for coming, John,' Father Parfitt says. 'I don't think I could have got through this morning without you.'

'Nonsense, Gideon,' the Archbishop replies. 'You underestimate the trust you have built with your congregation.'

'That's what made it so hard. Lying to them like that.'

'And what do you suggest? That we tell them the truth?'

'Surely that's what God would ask of us, John,' Father Parfitt says. 'That we at least tell the truth when we stand beneath his roof.'

'But this is not the Middle Ages. You can't be suggesting that we tell the people of Burnham All-Saints that the devil walks amongst them. We can't tell them the real reason why these girls have been taken. Come on, Gideon, they'd never understand!'

'You're right, John, put it down to a momentary lapse of faith. It's just sometimes I wonder how God will judge us at the end of this, when it's all said and done.'

'Gideon,' the Archbishop says, lowering his voice. 'You are God's soldier. He will see the suffering you

167

have endured. He will thank you for the difficult decisions that you have made along the way.'

'Thanks, John, I really mean it. Your words give me real comfort, just as they did the congregation this morning.'

'You know the clergymen of this diocese have kept this secret for over three hundred years,' the Archbishop says. 'You're not the first and I doubt you'll be the last to question the right and wrongs of it all.'

'I'll keep fighting the good fight. You can count on me.'

'That's the spirit. Keep up your patrols. I want you to take them well beyond the abbey itself. Make sure those who are guilty of witchcraft are uncovered, Gideon.'

'I will John, don't you worry,' Father Parfitt says. 'Now, let me see you out.'

I'm so lost in their conversation, it takes a second for Parfitt's words to sink in. Before I have a chance to move, the door creaks open. I stand up against the wall as it swings out towards me. Then I cling to the handle, praying they don't pull it back.

Safely hidden, I listen to them walk up the side chapel, poking my head out to see them turn back into the main body of the cathedral. Any shred of doubt that I may have had is now gone. Father Parfitt is definitely the man in white; I heard it with my own ears.

My thoughts are suddenly disturbed by a loud booming echo. It must be the cathedral door being closed. Then I hear Parfitt's footsteps returning towards me.

With nowhere to run, I dive into the vestry.

My eyes work their way around the room, looking for somewhere to hide. I hesitate a moment, shocked at what I see. The walls are covered in diagrams of torture devices. There's an old oak bookshelf in the corner, filled with dusty volumes all about witchcraft. At the other side there's an antique writing desk and strewn across it are documents written in old English.

It's like staring at the first few pages of Emily's book.

Parfitt's footsteps bound closer, and my heart quickens with them, like it's dancing in my chest. Then I notice the back window is slightly ajar. Frantically I wedge my fingers beneath its rotting frame, wrenching it open. The door handle rattles behind me. Then I pull myself up and out.

I run across the cathedral gardens and into the orchard, still not looking back. Then I cross the Bream and continue through the graveyard onto the chapel. I know it's still light and far too early for Emily to be there, but I need a safe place to get my head straight.

I'm relieved when the old iron ring turns and the chapel door falls open easily. I step inside and sit down in the back row to clear my thoughts. Leaning back, I look up at the ceiling – only two stone cherubs remain.

One is swinging from the roof beams by her hair and the other is posed like a crucifix, her feet bound together and her arms outstretched.

'I swear there used to be six of them,' a familiar voice says, startling me from the front row.

'Jack,' I say. 'What are you doing here?'

'Praying for a miracle,' he says, beckoning me over to sit next to him. 'I was really hoping I might see you here.'

'Really?' I say. 'You seemed a bit off with me at school the other day.'

'Yeah, I know. But your Mum called me last night and told me the news.'

'She did what? I can't believe she told you first. Was I going to be the last to know?'

There's a long pause as Jack holds his head low. His eyes become wet and his voice begins to crack. 'I'm just not ready for this,' he says. 'I'm not ready to say goodbye.'

'I know, Jack.' I say, putting my arm around him. 'I'm working on something. I can't tell you what, but you need to trust me. It's all going to be alright.'

'Do you promise?' Jack looks up at me like a child.

'I promise. But I need you to do something for me.'

'What? I'll do anything you want.'

'I need you to be there tomorrow,' I say. 'If I'm running late, just hold things up. Please, Jack, it's really important. Don't let them do anything before I get there.'

'I'll try,' he says, stroking my hand, which is now resting on his shoulder. 'But there's only so much I can do. I'm not family.'

Slowly he turns towards me. Our eyes meet and his face closes in on mine. 'You just look so much like her,' he says.

Then he pushes his lips together and presses them against mine.

'Jack! What are you doing?' I pull away and slap him hard around the face. 'Get off me!'

'Sorry,' he says, getting up and walking away up the aisle. 'I just thought...'

'Well, you thought wrong,' I say. 'I'm never going to forgive you for this, Jack.'

He slams the door behind him and I sit there awhile longer.

I just can't believe it.

First Mum, then Father Parfitt and now Jack. It's like everywhere I go today, someone has a nasty surprise waiting for me. All I really need is a moment of peace, a friendly face to turn to. I just need someone to take my side of things, someone to share the burden of my worries.

I really need Scarlett.

– Paige –

I don't know how long I sit alone inside the chapel, the events of the day rushing through my mind. The light begins to wane outside. I feel my eyelids grow heavy and at some point I drift off to sleep.

The chapel door flies open, waking me with a start. In bound Emily and the twins, followed by Alice, who is still naked beneath the red velvet blanket I tied around her neck last night.

'Rose, what are you doing here?' Emily says. 'I thought we were meeting under the bridge.'

'I had some bad news today,' I say. 'I didn't have anywhere else to go.'

'What is it?' Emily says. 'What's happened?'

'I don't know where to start. Do you want to know all of it or just the worst bits?'

'Just the worst bits,' the twins say. 'We haven't got all night and we've still got to give Alice a makeover before we go anywhere.'

'Ignore them,' Emily says. 'I want to know what's wrong. All of it.'

'Well, Jack tried to kiss me, I heard Parfitt make a full confession, but worst of all, they're going to turn off Scarlett's life-support in the morning. It's all over, Emily. There's no way in the world we can wake up both Hope and Paige, sort out Parfitt, get you and your sisters to the other side and send back Scarlett, all before tomorrow morning.'

'Why not?' Emily sits down and rests her arm around me. 'Paige is going to take time, I'll grant you that. But Hope is here in the abbey and so is your friend Father Parfitt. We've just got to make a plan, that's all.'

'So where should we start?'

'Well, you and I should head out to Badfield Ash to get Paige. The twins can stay here with Alice; they'll only slow us down anyway.'

'And the monks?' I say. 'How are we going to get past them to wake up Hope?'

'We're going to have to draw them away from the cathedral, that's for sure,' Emily says. 'It's probably going to get ugly. But we'll manage. Once we have a full coven of seven sisters, we'll lead the preacher man here to the chapel and open the gateway. Then we'll rest on the other side and send back Scarlett.'

'Do you think we can do all that tonight?'

'We have to,' Emily says. 'After all, you do know what tonight is?'

'Well,' I say, having to think awhile. 'If tomorrow is the first of November, then tonight is…'

'Halloween!' the twins say. 'It's our night.'

'That's right,' Emily says. 'The night when witches are at their most powerful.'

Alice and the twins give us a lift under the abbey walls on the Plot, whilst Emily packs her satchel with her beloved book. She slings me my crossbow with its

173

few remaining arrows and then we get off beneath the Humping Monks, just as the church bells chime midnight.

'We'll be back by two,' Emily says to the twins. 'In the meantime, take a look around the abbey to get a headcount on the monks. But don't do anything stupid. Remember we need a full coven of seven sisters by the end of the night.'

'Understood,' the twins say. 'Is there time to give Alice her makeover too?'

'I guess so,' Emily says. 'But be here for two.'

Emily and I climb up onto street level and look around the market square for any sign of Parfitt. A full moon swelters in the sky, making it seem like dusk. But there's not a soul in sight. There isn't even a light on in the Angel.

'It's all clear,' I say, turning towards Emily. 'I guess the rumour of a killer on the loose has kept the *trick or treaters* at home.'

'We don't need any living people. We just need a horse or something to come through, so we can get to Badfield and back by two.'

'What about Billy's friend on the milk wagon? By rights he should be here any moment.'

'Good thinking,' Emily says. 'Load up your bow and let's get outside the abbey gate ready for him.'

'Surely there's no need for that. If he's a friend of Billy's, he'll probably just give us a lift.'

'We'll do what we have to,' Emily says. 'For our sisters' sake.'

I do as she says, loading up and then hanging my bow over my back. A few moments later, the old wagon comes rolling over the Humping Monks, pulled along by a scruffy little piebald no bigger than a pony. I've never noticed him before, but the driver is young, and fairly good looking too, with curly dark hair and bright blue eyes.

'Hey there, handsome,' Emily says, walking out into the road, forcing the driver to pull on the reins and make a stop. 'Room for two more?'

'Not really. I've been delivering since dawn and my bed has been calling out to me for over an hour.'

Emily removes her satchel from her shoulder, giving me a sideways look that I instantly understand.

'Come on,' I say, resisting the temptation to draw my bow. 'We're friends of Billy's.'

'Billy who?' the driver says.

'Billy Tanner,' I say. 'I saw him get off your wagon a couple of nights ago.'

'Oh, that guy,' the driver says. 'I barely know him. To be honest he still owes me money for the ride. Said he was going to pay up tomorrow, but he never did. I only agreed to take him because it was on my way to Walsham.'

'Did you say Walsham?' I ask. 'It's just we want to get to Badfield Ash. It's only a couple of miles from Walsham.'

175

'It's probably even less,' the driver says. 'But I don't like to stop in Badfield. Nobody likes to stop in Badfield.'

'Just slow down then,' Emily says, fluttering her eyelashes at him sweetly. 'We'll jump out whilst you're still moving; you'll not even know we're there.'

'Oh, go on then. But if you see your friend Tanner, remind him he still owes me a penny.'

'Of course we will,' I say, smiling. 'We'll tell him he owes you two.'

We sit on two long benches beneath a curved canvas roof, which has a large tear running across its breadth. The sound of hooves striking the road is deafening and the rickety wooden wheels do nothing to absorb the bumps.

I see the central square disappear behind us, followed by the traffic lights. I wait until the driver looks preoccupied before tugging on Emily's dress. 'How are we going to get back?' I say, keeping my voice low. 'It's got to be two hours walk at the least.'

'Don't worry, I'll read him a story before I put him to sleep,' Emily says, pulling her book out of her satchel and then tilting her head sideways.

'If you really must, but go easy on him,' I say. 'Why do you think he was so scared to stop at Badfield, anyway?'

'Don't you know?' Emily says. 'I thought everyone knew about Badfield Ash.'

'Knew what?'

176

'Well, they call it Badfield Ash because it got burnt down during the Black Death. They did it to rid the land of disease.'

'So what?'

'People say it's been cursed ever since,' Emily says. 'Nothing grows there. Nobody lived there, not in the old village, not when I was alive. That's why the preacher man chose it as the place to burn Paige. So her soul would have to rest there for eternity.'

'Were you burnt there too?'

'No. He led the three of us there: Paige, Hope and me. He said he'd spare Hope if we both confessed. I knew he was lying, but Paige, she confessed. She did it to protect Hope.'

'Hope was the youngest, wasn't she?'

'We found her on the steps of Burnham All-Saints Chapel,' Emily says. 'She was no more than three on the day she died and we'd practically raised her from birth. That's why we called her Hope; she was our hope for the future. We'd have all done anything to protect her, but I knew he couldn't be trusted. Someone had to keep themselves alive, to watch over her.'

'You were right,' I say. 'Surely Paige could see that.'

'Try telling Paige that.'

'What happened to her anyway?'

'He tied her by her hair to the only tree in Badfield,' Emily says. 'Then he lit a fire beneath it and watched her suffer, waiting until her hair burnt or the branch

177

snapped before she fell into the flames. And do you know what her last words were?'

'No idea. Something to you, telling you to watch over Hope?'

'You would think so, wouldn't you?' Emily says. 'As she fell into the fire, she told me to go to hell. She probably still blames me now.'

'I'm sure she doesn't,' I say.

'You don't know Paige. She used to work the land before she came to the chapel. She's as hard as frozen soil and as stubborn as a goat.'

'It was a long time ago. Surely she's gotten over it by now.'

'I don't think so. In fact, I know so.'

There's a painful silence between us for the next mile or so. Emily skims through the pages of her book, whilst I look out of the back of the trailer. We pass a row of trees that line both sides of the road, their branches stretching out and joining up like long, bony fingers. Then all of a sudden they come to a stop and the wayside becomes wasted and barren. I feel the wagon slow down and Emily frantically packs the book back into her bag.

'Anytime now, ladies,' the driver says. 'I'm not slowing down anymore.'

'Okay,' I say, standing up, making as much noise about it as possible. 'We're going now.'

Emily presses her index finger to her lip, sneaking up behind the driver. Then she swirls her bag above her head and hits him clean on the back of the neck, knocking him out cold.

'Come on,' she says, as he slumps forward on his seat. 'Help me drag him into the back.'

We lay him out on his side in the recovery position, whilst the little horse comes to halt in the middle of the road. We realise that there's nothing to tie him up to, so Emily gets the idea of taking off the driver's belt and using it to brake the trailer, by strapping one of the wheels to an iron nail poking out the side.

'That should hold it,' she says.

Then we head off into Badfield, both hoping that the horse and cart are still there waiting when we return. There are a couple of cottages up ahead, both painted in traditional Suffolk pink, but neither really looks inhabited. I know there's a shop a mile up the road and a village pub too, but Emily doesn't take us that far, skipping through a field instead.

Long stalks of corn sprout waist height from the ground. It's strange to see them not harvested this time of year, but then again, they look wilted and decayed, as if they've stood in this state for many years. I let them sway beneath my fingers as I hurry to keep up with Emily, whose eyes are narrowed on a strange shadow on the horizon.

As we get closer, I can see that it's a church. It's even scarier looking than Emily's chapel back in Burnham. There's no pathway leading up to it, and no graveyard either. It just sits there, alone and abandoned in the middle of a field. The windows and doors have been boarded up and grotesque gargoyles spit down thin wet ribbons, even though it hasn't rained since last night's storm.

'What is this place?' I gasp.

'The old church,' Emily says. 'It was in the centre of the village before they burnt it down. Paige's tree is just behind it.'

We press on a couple of hundred yards more towards an old oak tree, its evil shadow elongated by the low moon. Long wretched branches scrape at the sky and the thick trunk is blackened by ash.

'We're here,' Emily says, taking out her book and sitting on the ground. 'Let's get this done and get out of here.'

'Agreed,' I say, looking up at the twisted tree. 'I can see why nobody wants to stop here now.'

We join hands on the cover of the book and Emily begins to make the chant. 'I channel the Earth in the name of my sisters. Air, soil, water and fire, let my sisters wake.'

We say it together, over and over.

'Sorores in Aeternum!' Emily screams, raising our hands off the cover of the book.

Storm clouds brew overhead. Then lightning strikes the tree and a body falls from its branches. Emily and I stand up together, still holding hands as the figure rises before us. Her hair is short and twisted, her face charred black. But even below her burnt rags, I can see that she's thickset and muscular.

'Paige, is that you?' Emily says.

'Who else?' she replies. 'Who's that with you?'

'This is Rose. She's one of us now. She's our seventh sister.'

'And Hope?' Paige says, coming in close. 'Where is she?'

'I can explain,' Emily says, holding up her hands. 'I'm here to put it right.'

Paige grabs Emily by the throat and thrusts her against the tree. I try to get between them, but Paige brushes me aside easily with her other hand, sending me to the ground.

'Rose,' Emily says, choking. 'Go and get the horse and trailer ready. Give me and Paige a moment to sort this out.'

I get back onto my feet and slowly step away, watching as Emily prises Paige's hand away from her neck. They continue in a heated exchange, Paige trying to get hold of Emily again, but Emily giving as good as she gets.

'Are you sure you're alright?' I say.

'Just go,' Emily says. 'We'll be there in a minute.'

I do as I'm told and leave them to it, quickening my pace as I pass the deserted church. Halfway across the cornfield, I catch sight of the horse and cart, still in the middle of the road, and for a moment I feel relieved.

But then I hear voices.

181

Turning around, I see a crowd of children running and laughing. In a matter of seconds they overtake me. Their hands link together and they start to walk around me in a circle.

Ring-a-ring o' roses,
A pocket full of posies,
A-tishoo! A-tishoo!
We all fall down.

They all tumble to the ground laughing, their hands still joined together and their legs stretched out wide. I try to step over a small boy and continue on to the trailer, but he jumps up and blocks my way.

Standing up, he's no higher than my waist, with thick brown hair and light coloured eyes. He wraps his arms around my thighs, pushing his head against my hip. Then he pulls his face away and I see that it's bleeding.

'What's wrong with you?' I say, kneeling down before him. 'We need to get you a bandage.'

Then I notice the others have stood up too. They're all closing in on me, and they all have open sores spread across their faces.

'We're hungry!' they say, opening their mouths to reveal sharp fanged teeth. 'We need to eat.'

The boy in front of me sinks his teeth into my cheek. I put my hands on his shoulders trying to push him away, but he's so strong. Eventually I force myself free, but I end up falling over backwards. Suddenly there must be twenty of them, stood over me, their teeth glistening in the moonlight.

Then I see Emily's satchel catch one on the back of the head and Paige muscles her way through, pulling me to my feet. 'Come on!' she says. 'Let's go!'

We run through the long strands of corn towards the trailer. I look back to see Emily a few strides behind, one of the children still clinging around her ankle. She kicks out wildly. He flies off and is trampled on by the chasing crowd.

'Who are they?' I pant.

'There's no time to explain,' Emily says, overtaking me. 'Just get in the back of that wagon as soon as you can.'

Paige pulls on ahead and takes the driver's seat. Emily arrives next and frantically unclasps the belt from around the wheel. Then she leaps on board and Paige cracks the reins, startling the little horse into life.

Emily holds out her hand. 'Rose,' she screams. 'Hurry up!'

I feel the children's breath on the back of my neck. I jump onto the trailer and fall flat on my face beside the driver. Then I sit up straight to see the children still chasing us. The one who bit me is even holding onto the back of the trailer and pulling himself up.

'They won't give up now they've got a taste of blood,' Paige says. 'You'd better do something and do it fast!'

Emily kicks the light-eyed child straight in the face and he falls to the ground. Then she grabs the driver's lifeless body, tightening her fingers through the belt loops of his loosely fitting trousers.

'Emily, no!' I shout. 'It's not his fault. You can't…' But it's too late.

She throws him from the back and he cartwheels to the ground. The children stop chasing and swarm around him. I try to close my eyes, but I can't. He sits bolt upright for a moment, fear etched across his face. Then he lets out a long piercing scream as they start to rip the flesh from his bones.

We barely say a word for the next mile or two. I keep my head buried in my hands, unable to get the vision of the driver's face out of my head. We must be halfway back to Burnham before Emily comes to sit beside me, wiping away at the wound below my left eye.

'I know,' I say, before she even has a chance to speak. 'You did it for our sisters.'

'It was him or us, Rose,' Emily says. 'They wouldn't have stopped and there's no way we could have outrun them. We couldn't have galloped away into the night on that sad little excuse for a horse. Not all three of us.'

'But it's not forever is it?' I ask. 'He'll be right as rain tomorrow. Won't he?'

'I'm afraid not,' Emily says, shaking her head. 'They took his soul, just like Silas did to Fourfingers.'

'Who the hell are they?'

'Ghost eaters,' Emily says. 'Sometimes when many people are killed, all in one place, in a really horrible way, they come back as ghost eaters.'

'So what happened to them? None of them could have been any older than six or seven.'

'They were the children of the village,' Emily says. 'The one they burnt down.'

'Where were their parents? Why were there only children left?'

'Well, from what I heard it wasn't the people of Badfield Ash that burnt down the village. It was the people of Walsham and the neighbouring villages. They came down in the night with torches and raised the place to the ground. They did it to stop the spread of Black Death. But one of the farmers knew what was coming and he locked the children in the local church, the one you saw boarded up. He supposedly put up a fight, but there were too many of them. The story goes that nobody found out about the children, not until it was too late, anyway. They must have died there in the church – long drawn-out deaths of infection and disease, with no parents to care for them, nothing.'

'That's the most horrible thing I've ever heard,' I say, pushing her away. 'No wonder their souls are angry.'

'Well, I guess that's the difference between us,' Emily says. 'Your world is all sweetness and light. The only thing you and your sister ever had to worry about is down to your own stupidity. My life wasn't like that!'

'Hey, come on Emily,' I say. 'That's not fair.'

'Isn't it?'

Tears start streaming down her cheeks and although I've seen her cry before, this time it's different. For the first time since we got the book out from the museum, she looks frail and weak.

'Look, I'm sorry, it's been a long day and a rough night,' I say, putting my arm around her. 'You know, you never did tell me how it finished up with you and Hope.'

'Didn't I? Are you sure you want to hear it? Are you sure it won't be too horrible for you?'

'Of course I want to hear it. After all we *are* sisters now, aren't we?'

'I guess so.' Emily wipes away her tears.

'So I take it, things didn't end well. Or we wouldn't be here, would we?'

'That's right,' Emily says, her eyes bloodshot and her nose running. 'He tied Hope to the cross outside the abbey the following day.'

'Surely he didn't burn her,' I say. 'She was just a child.'

'No, he killed her quickly. He staked her through the chest. Then he dragged me right up close and made me look. Making sure it was the last thing that I ever saw.'

'And then what?' I say.

'Then he burnt my eyes out with a hot poker. He let me wander around the abbey blind, with people throwing sticks and flints at me, so I could be a reminder to everyone about the dangers of witchcraft. Eventually I died of infection, somewhere near the chapel. I don't know when. I don't even know where.'

'You know, you were right about life being easier for me,' I say. 'And what happened to you and Hope, that was every bit as horrible as those kids dying out at Badfield Ash. Probably even worse.'

'But it's not your fault is it? And thanks to you, tonight we're finally going to put things right.'

– Fight for Your Sisters –

We leave the old milk wagon right outside the abbey gate and run the last few metres across the Humping Monks. The church bells chime two as we hurry down the steps onto the towpath, relieved to see the Plot there waiting for us. Madelyn is at the helm in her grey fur coat, one hand on the wheel and the other waving out towards us.

'Paige,' she screams excitedly. 'You're never going to guess what we've done whilst you've been gone.'

'It's been three hundred years,' Paige says. 'This could take a while.'

'No,' Evelyn says, poking her head up from the hold. 'She means tonight. Come and see.'

We squeeze through the hatch and shimmy down the stairs, gathering in the long galley-shaped room below deck. Standing there right in front of the stove is Alice. She's still wearing the red blanket I gave her last night, but now she has a black corset on beneath it and the twins have cut up a fur coat to make her a pair of hot-pants and matching knee-high boots.

'Alice look pretty,' she says, with a big grin on her face.

'Yes, Alice looks *really* pretty,' Emily says. 'I hope you two found time to spy on the enemy too.'

'Don't you like it?' the twins say. 'It took us nearly two hours.'

'You're not only guilty of witchcraft,' I say. 'You can add crimes against fashion to your record now too.'

'Good one,' Paige says, laughing loudly. 'Maybe Emily was right about you after all.'

We continue on up the Bream, Emily guiding the Plot beneath the abbey walls and mooring us up under the footbridge by the cathedral orchard. The twins lead Alice up on deck, both still beaming about their creation. Paige emerges out of the hatch last of all. She's now dressed in a leopard print coat and is carrying a few empty bottles, which she stands up on the deck.

'Right, let's get this started,' she says, pulling us all into a circle. 'Me, Alice and the twins are going to stay here in the trees and get ready for the monks. Rose and Emily, I want you to make a loop around the moat. We need to know numbers.'

'Who died and made you in charge?' Emily says.

'Well, we all died when you we're in charge,' Paige replies. 'So now it's my turn.'

There's a tense silence between them. Then Paige pulls out a knife from her pocket and starts scraping a deep gouge into the wooden deck boards around the bottles.

'Alice is going to dig a trench in the trees,' she says. 'Together we'll line it with sharp spikes and cover it over with leaves. Then we'll draw the monks into us. It'll take at least five of us to hold the line, but whatever happens we can't allow them outflank us.'

She pauses to make sure we're keeping up before she continues.

'Rose, I want you to hold back and pick them off with your bow. We can't afford to let them get in close to you. You're still alive and we want to keep you that way. Only when every last one of those monks is dead can we go up to the cathedral and wake up Hope. Does everybody understand?'

'Me dig,' Alice says.

'We'll hold the line,' the twins say.

'And I'll hang back and pick them off with my bow,' I say.

'That's the spirit,' Paige says. 'Emily, are you in?'

'I'm in,' she says reluctantly. 'But watch out for the man in white. Even the six of us together can't take him. If he appears, then we'll have to fall back to the chapel and make another plan.'

'Agreed,' Paige says. 'And nobody get any ideas about being a hero. I know you're all dead and you'll be right as rain by the morning, but we need to finish this tonight, with all our sisters intact.'

Emily and I watch awhile as Alice starts to dig just inside the tree-line. No sooner does her foot strike the lug than her shovel cuts deep into the ground and sprays earth up over her shoulder. I've never seen anyone dig quite like it. Paige pulls off several large spear-sized branches from the trees and the twins sit in the middle, whittling the ends to make them sharp.

'Come on,' Emily says, untying the Plot from the bridge. 'Let's get going.'

'No problem,' I say. 'But are you sure you're alright?'

'Of course. Why wouldn't I be?'

'I mean with Paige. You we're right about her being headstrong.'

'I know,' Emily says. 'She drives me crazy, but she means well.'

'She reminds me a bit of Scarlett,' I say. 'She always used to boss me about. I hated her for it. Sometimes I even think it's my fault what happened to her, you know.'

'Why? You didn't push her off that wall.'

'I know. But when I think of every time that I was less than patient with her, every time I was jealous, or wished that just for once somebody would notice me. Maybe part of me wanted her to fall.'

'That's not why it happened,' Emily says, giving me a hug. 'And she'll be awake this time tomorrow, all because of you.'

'Because of us!' I say.

We chug along the Bream, keeping our distance so not to be spotted. From the safety of the Plot, we look across at the abbey ruins. There's at least six monks gathered in the open-air cloisters, deep in conversation. Two more kneel in a small chamber just off it, whilst another four make their way through the grand archway of the boarding house.

191

'I make that twelve,' Emily says. 'Any more?'

'Nope,' I say. 'Let's go and check the cathedral.'

We continue on the river until it disappears beneath the abbey walls, then we bear left, keeping to the moat.

We squeeze below the drawbridge in front of the Norman Tower and slow down just a hundred yards shy of the cathedral.

Large gothic archways scale its tall turreted tower, which must be visible from every inch of the abbey estate. Several spotlights trail their way up its walls, firmly focused on four steel crosses crowning its four corners.

'This is it,' Emily says. 'This is their stronghold.'

'How do we know how many are inside?' I say.

'Pass me your crossbow.' Emily aims over the top of the steering wheel. 'I've got an idea.'

She lets fire and the arrow strikes the huge oak doors and stops with a shudder. We watch from the shadows of the perimeter wall as the cathedral doors are flung open and two orderly rows of monks flood down the steps.

Some of them are young and sturdy-looking, in their mid-thirties. But there are others who seem old and frail. Together they gather at the bottom of the steps holding wooden torches, most of which are yet to be lit.

Then they break ranks and begin to form little groups, making them almost impossible to count.

'How many do you make it?' I say, turning to Emily.

'I got to at least forty. With the others back there, that makes…'

'Fifty-two,' I say. 'Can we take that many?'

'That's getting on for ten to one,' Emily says, her eyes focused ahead. 'It's going to be tough. But we do have the full moon on our side and it *is* Halloween.'

We both pause for a moment, weighing up our chances.

'At least we haven't seen the man in white,' Emily says.

'Hopefully we won't either,' I say. 'I heard the Archbishop tell him to take his patrols further afield tonight.'

'Let's pray we can get Hope back before he returns,' Emily says.

'Come on,' I say, pushing forward on the big brass lever beside the steering wheel. 'Let's get to the others and tell them what we're up against.'

We duck down low, continuing along the side of the cathedral. Then we take a sharp left as the moat curves past the tunnel where we first entered the abbey. With our circle complete, we moor up amongst the trees, just as the church bells strike three.

Somehow Alice has finished the trench, which is now fifty feet long and curls in a semi-circle back to the river. The twins have mucked in too, knee-deep in mud, lining the trench with stakes.

'Good work, Alice,' I say, jumping down onto dry land. 'How did you do it so quick?'

'Alice loves to dig,' she says, a broad grin across her muddied face.

'What about us?' the twins say, pulling themselves out of the trench and then helping Alice up to join us.

'You did well too. But how are we going to get it covered?'

'For that we're going to need a little help from the Earth,' Paige says.

The six of us sit in a circle, right in the middle of the trees. Emily lays her satchel on the floor and pulls out the book of human skin. Then we all rest our hands on the cover, joining them at the fingertips.

'I channel the Earth in the name of my sisters,' we say together. 'Air, soil, water and fire.'

Over and over, we chant, each time a little more loudly than before.

'Ventis Onis!' Emily says, breaking the chorus and screaming at the top of her voice.

A fierce wind picks up, shaving the trees of their remaining leaves. Then it starts to twist through the naked branches, howling as it goes. The leaves dance around us, spinning like a cyclone, before coming to rest in the trench, covering it over and hiding the stakes.

'Now to get their attention,' Paige says, urging us all to put our hands back in the middle.

'I channel the Earth in the name of my sisters,' we say together. 'Air, soil, water and fire.'

Over and over again.

194

'Ignis Orbitas,' Paige says, taking her hands off the book and raising them to the sky.

A circle of fire leaps up around the trench, at least ten inches high. We all jump to our feet, the light from the flames stretching our shadows amongst the trees.

'So how many are we looking at?' Paige says.

'Fifty,' Emily says. 'Maybe more.'

Dozens of torches appear at the back of the cathedral and slowly they begin to group together. The monks order themselves in a square formation, standing before a giant wooden cross. A loud thumping fills the air and a few more monks join at the back, beating on huge wooden drums. Then they all break into song, chanting in some ancient language.

'Remember what we're fighting for?' Paige says. 'We're doing this for Hope.'

A loud horn is sounded and the front line of monks advances towards us. I see the whites of their eyes and the silver crucifixes hanging from their necks.

'Hold the line,' Paige says sternly.

Everyone steps forward to the edge of the trench. The twins are clutching spears. Emily is holding her satchel containing her heavy book, swinging it wildly around her head. And Alice has her shovel raised, ready for action.

'Rose, drop back and load your bow,' Paige orders.

The monks bound forward, their footsteps thumping the ground like a herd of galloping horses.

'Everybody hold,' Paige cries. 'Wait for my command.'

The first wave is right upon us. Their hoods are flung back, their faces are filled with anger and there are burning torches held tightly in their hands. They breach the circle of fire, just a few feet from the trench.

'Now!' Paige shouts. 'Sisters fall back!'

All together the girls take a single step back. The monks fall into the deep gully and the air is filled with screams of pain. The monks' thick frames fall onto the spikes and one by one they become impaled.

'It won't work again,' Paige says, as another horn sounds and the next wave of monks begins their approach. 'Sisters, step up to the line!' she screams. 'Rose, fire at will!'

I hold my crossbow over my forearm to stop it shaking. Then I let fly. I catch a monk in the stomach and he falls to the ground. The one next to him stops to see if he's alright and I hit him straight between the eyes. Claret gushes down his face and he keels forward onto his stomach, sending the arrow right through his skull and out the other side.

Two more monks try to break the line in the middle, but Alice meets them with her shovel, battering them both to the ground and continuing to pound their bodies. Emily strikes another one in the chest with her satchel, forcing him to fall back. He topples over into the gully and a spike appears through the front of his cloak. His eyes remain open, but his tongue falls out of his mouth and blood dribbles down his chin.

One manages to get through on my left side and he takes down Paige, knocking the spear clear from her hands. They roll around on the ground. First he's on top, trying to strangle her, but then she rolls him off and starts gouging out his eyes.

Everything becomes blurred for a moment- I'm surrounded by figures fighting amongst the trees.

Then I catch sight of the twins in trouble on the right flank. Two monks lie speared to the ground either side of them, but a third one is moving in, his torch swinging in front of him. I narrow my eyes, waiting for a clear shot. My hand is shaking – I worry that I might hit Evelyn by mistake.

I let rip. My arrow whistles past her shoulder, striking the monk clean on the thigh. He drops his torch and falls to his knees. Madelyn doesn't hesitate, rushing over and putting a choke-hold on him from behind. Then Evelyn picks up his torch and teases the flame across his face.

The horn sounds again and the remaining monks begin to fall back, making a desperate run for the wooden cross behind the cathedral. I take the last few arrows left in my quiver, and I let it rain, shooting them in the back as they scurry up the hill like rats.

Then I step forward and gather in the centre of the circle with my sisters. The full moon of Halloween beams down on us as we stand there surrounded by blood and bodies. There must be twenty of them, piled up in the trench, broken limbs pointing in all directions and jagged spikes poking through their torn cloaks.

Ten more lie on our side of the line, their eyes still open, but the life beaten out of their battered corpses. Another ten line the hill that runs up towards the cathedral. It's an absolute massacre, blood running so thick that it curdles on the banks of the Bream and turns the water red.

'Well fought, sisters!' Emily screams. 'But it's not over yet – we still need to take the cross. That's where he killed Hope.'

'Don't be too hasty,' Paige says. 'Fighting in the trees has been working out for us.'

Emily and Paige square up to each other in the centre. Paige puts her hands on Emily's elbows and squeezes them into her sides, trying to make her listen. But Emily shrugs her off easily. Her red hair in a giant frizz, burning beneath the full moon, and her pretty green eyes are filled with rage.

'Remember the reason why they fight us,' she says, slinging her satchel over her shoulder and picking up a spear that's been stabbed into a monk's stomach. 'They hunt us out of fear.'

'She's right,' the twins say, joining her in arms. 'They're terrified of us.'

'We fight for our sisters,' Emily says, beckoning Alice towards her. 'For three hundred years, they've drowned us, burnt us and squeezed the life from our bones. Well, tonight, under the full moon of Halloween, we will have our revenge!'

'Come on, Paige,' I say, throwing my empty crossbow onto the ground and replacing it with a spear. 'Let's finish this.'

The church bells strike four as we leap across the trench, spears in hand, running through the dying embers of the circle of fire. Our feet strike the ground and kick up sod and turf. Twelve monks are circled around the cross and although they outnumber us two to one, the closer we get, the smaller they look.

They cower backwards in a huddle, each one trying not to be at the front when we arrive. I look them up and down, noticing that the remaining few are grey-haired and leather-skinned. Most of them are unarmed, even their drums and horns lay strewn across the ground.

We meet them in a perfect line, all six sisters at the same time, hitting them hard. I drive my spear through the first one I meet, staking him into the sticky soil. Each of my sisters does the same.

'We pray for your mercy,' one at the back says, his head bowed. 'God will forgive you.'

Emily keeps running and kicks him straight in the face. Paige knocks another one to the ground and starts stamping on his head. Alice pounds a third one with her shovel, whilst Evelyn and Madelyn both have one between their thighs, scratching out their eyes.

I stand there and watch; there is nothing left to do as my sisters continue to punish them. Three hundred years of hatred is slowly vented.

It must go on for several minutes before everybody begins to slow down, exhausted, and stops what they're doing.

'This is it,' Emily says. 'We just need Hope now.'

Circled around the wooden cross, we begin to congratulate each other. Paige comes over and slaps me hard on the back. Then she wraps her arms around Emily, lifting her feet off the floor. The twins give each other a high-five, before looking around for Alice.

Then, out of the corner of my eye, I see one of the monks struggle to his feet. He lifts up his cloak and removes a dagger from a garter tied around his thigh. Everything slows down. I try to say something.

But I can't.

His hand goes up above his head and then, with his last breath, he drives the knife into Alice's back just below her shoulder blade.

She stumbles to the ground. The monk falls down on top of her. Everybody stops what they're doing; nobody is able to speak.

We just stand there, looking at them both in a tangled heap on the ground.

– Hope –

'Oh my God,' I scream. 'Alice!'

Paige and Emily bend down and roll the monk's lifeless body off Alice's back. But Alice doesn't move. The knife is still stuck into the flesh just below her shoulder blade and her face is pressed down into the mud.

'Alice, can you hear us?' The twins crouch down in front of her. 'Are you alright?'

Alice raises her chin, her eyes weary and distant. 'Alice, hurt. Alice hurt really bad.'

'I told you this was a bad idea,' Paige says, standing up over Alice's body and flaring up at Emily. 'We came out of the trees too early. This is your fault!'

'Well, if it wasn't for me, none of us would be here,' Emily says, standing her ground. 'And you'd still be burning in hell.'

'Both of you stop it,' I say. 'For Alice's sake. She needs us to be strong.'

'She's right,' the twins say, tearing strips from the dead monk's cloak. 'Somebody's got to pull that blade out so we can dress the wound.'

'I'll do it,' Emily says. 'Paige, you hold her legs.'

'No, you hold her legs,' Paige says. 'I'll get the blade out.'

'For God's sake!' I shout. 'I'll hold her legs. Just get on with pulling that knife out.'

Paige crouches down at Alice's head, stroking the long hair that runs down her spine. The twins hover over us, holding torn strips of cloth. Then Emily puts her foot right in the small of Alice's back and grabs the knife by the handle.

'On three,' she says, steadying herself. 'One, two, three!'

There's a loud scream that rings through the abbey ruins and probably carries all the way back to the chapel. Alice peels her head off the ground, her face twisted with pain. Then Emily and Paige take an arm each and pull her up onto her knees.

The twins get to work. Together they bind Alice up the best they can, wrapping the strips of material right around the broadest part of her back and tying them tightly around her bust.

'It couldn't be in a more awkward place,' Evelyn says, shaking her head. 'We're going to need some alcohol for the pain and it's going to need stitching.'

'We've got some thread left in the Plot,' Madelyn says.

'There might be a bit of moonshine left too,' Emily adds.

'Right, I'll swing by and get it,' Paige says. 'Twins, see if you can get her to her feet. Then take her to the mausoleum by the chapel. She should be able to draw some strength from there, it's our land.'

'Good thinking,' Emily says. 'Me and Rose will wake up Hope and see you down there.'

202

The twins brace themselves either side of Alice and Paige leads them down towards the Bream. Emily and I watch over them until they disappear into the trees, before we turn our attention to the ten-foot wooden cross beside us.

Surrounded by slaughtered monks, Emily pulls out the book of human skin and lays it on the ground. Then we join our hands on its cover and begin chanting for the final time.

'I channel the Earth in the name of my sisters. Air, soil, water and fire, let my sisters wake.'

Over and over we say it.

'Sorores in Aeternum!' Emily screams, breaking her hands free.

The sound of crying rings loudly in my ears and the naked body of a toddler appears tied to the cross. Emily frantically unbinds her hands and pulls Hope down towards her chest, almost bringing the cross down too.

'It's alright,' Emily says, as Hope continues to cry. 'Your sisters are here now.'

Slowly the tears stop falling and I catch a glimpse of Hope's face as she peels it away from Emily's cleavage. She has loose curls of golden hair, plump cheeks and pretty eyes somewhere between blue and green. A smile stretches across her face, which must be infectious, because it instantly spreads onto Emily's face.

'What?' Emily says, noticing my expression.

'You look kind of sweet together,' I say. 'You could almost pass as her mother.'

'Yeah, right,' Emily laughs. 'Could you see me at home playing happy families?'

'Who knows? Maybe, if you'd been born into another time.'

'Trust me,' Emily says, placing Hope down onto her feet and gently smacking her bare bum. 'I'm much better at playing the wicked witch.'

Hope comes bounding over towards me, a little unsteady on her feet. She takes my hand and pulls me down to her level. 'Who are you? Do you know my big sister Paige?'

'Yes, I know Paige' I say, taking off my fur body-warmer and helping her to put it on. 'I know all of your sisters.'

'Are they here?' Hope says, pulling up the hood.

'Yes, they're here,' I say. 'Just a few minutes away.'

She's so cute, drowned in fur, my body-warmer far too long for her and dragging along the ground. Emily comes running over to help, tearing off the strap from her satchel and fastening it around Hope's middle as a belt.

'That's better,' Emily says, pinching Hope's rosy cheeks. 'As snug as a bug in a rug.'

'So can I see them?' Hope screams excitedly. 'Are the twins here?'

'They're all here,' I say. 'Alice too.'

'Come on then.' Hope grabs me by the hand. 'What are we waiting for?'

'Me!' a voice shouts from behind us.

We turn to see a man standing at the back of cathedral. He's holding a bible in one hand and a burning torch in the other. His long white gown is almost glowing in the bright spotlights and his tall pointed hat casts a shadow right across his face.

'Come on, Emily!' I shout. 'Let's go and get the others.'

'No,' she says, resting her shoulders beneath the arms of the cross. 'I think we can finish this one now.'

I hesitate a moment.

Then I let go of Hope's hand and join Emily on the other side of the cross. Together we pull it from the ground, letting it topple forward, so that the top is sticking out like a battering ram. Then, as if we'd read each other's mind, we charge straight for him.

The man in white stands firm, holding his bible up like a shield. The gold cross on its leather cover glistens in the light. His torch burns above his head.

We run right through him. The blunt end of the cross strikes him hard in the sternum. There's a loud crunching noise, like the breaking of ribs. He bends double, wedged onto the end of the cross. Then we drive him against the jagged flint-stone wall of the cathedral.

His arms flop down by his sides. The leather bible spills onto the ground, but his flame-lit torch still hangs loosely between his fingers. The tall white hat slips off his head and his mouth droops open. I look into his eyes, watching them fall shut.

'It's not him,' I say. 'It's not Parfitt!'

'I don't care!' Emily says, prising the torch from his hand.

I run back towards Hope, pushing her head into my stomach so she doesn't have to see. Looking over my shoulder, I catch Emily's face. Her green eyes are almost turning red under the burning light of the fire. She doesn't even flinch, dousing the old man's smock with his own torch. He lets out a long scream, his final breath. Then he falls quiet and the only sound remaining is the crackling of flames.

'Emily!' I shout. 'For God's sake, that's enough. It's not even Parfitt.'

'Are you sure?' Emily says, dropping the torch into the blaze and slowly turning towards us. 'He was wearing white.'

'So, maybe there are two of them? You said it yourself. It would need all seven of us to take him down. You said we'd have to open the gateway to hell.'

'You could be right,' Emily says, picking up her book from the ground. 'Let's not wait around to find out. Let's go and see if they've patched up Alice.'

'Come on,' Hope says. 'I want to see my sisters.'

The three of us run down the gentle slope towards the cathedral orchard, Emily and I on either side and Hope in the middle. I try my best to block Hope's view of what's around her. A trench three deep with dismembered bodies, corpses scattered in every direction and blood draining out into the Bream.

The church bells strike five as we make it through the graveyard and the chapel appears in front of us. We hurry around the tower, little Hope dragging us both along by our wrists.

Paige is there waiting for us when we arrive. She's standing on the island just in front of the mausoleum. I can make out Alice's feet poking from the doorway and two shadows on either side of her, which must be the twins.

'Hope, Hope! Is that you?' Paige shouts.

'Paige!' Hope cries, screaming with excitement.

'Give me a second, I'll come and get you on the raft,' Paige says, running over to the water's edge.

'Are the twins there?' Hope says.

'We're here,' two voices say, coming from the mausoleum.

'How's Alice?' I ask.

'She's alright,' Paige says, leaning forward and pulling the little wooden raft towards her. 'A bit dazed, but she'll be fine.'

Just then a figure of a man appears at the end of the pathway leading to the old rectory. He's wearing the same white smock as that of the man Emily's just burnt behind the cathedral. He holds the same leather bible, with an identical gold cross glistening on the cover. The only difference is the torchlight in his other hand. It's the modern type, with a bulb and batteries.

We all stop what we're doing. Paige is frozen, one foot dipped in the lake. The twins are still huddled around Alice's feet at the doorway of the mausoleum and Hope is exposed, standing by the water's edge.

Emily is the only one to react, running over to Hope and grabbing her by the hand. Then she comes back for me and drags us both through the chapel door.

'What are you doing?' I say frantically. 'You know he's got a set of keys.'

'I'm buying us some time,' she says. 'We'll climb out of the window at the back.'

'Then what?' I say, following her up the aisle, dragging Hope along with me.

'Whilst he's fumbling around here looking for us in the dark,' Emily says, prising open the rotting window frame, 'we'll come back in the front door with the others and force him through the gateway.'

'Good thinking,' I say, giving her a boost up onto the window ledge.

'Now for Hope,' Emily says, holding her hands up on the other side.

I lift up Hope and pass her to Emily through the open window.

'What about me?' I say, as the door rattles open behind me. 'I need a hand up too!'

Emily puts Hope safely down on the floor and then raises up her arms, her pretty green eyes staring deeply into mine. 'Sorry, Rose. It's real sisters only, from here on in!'

Then she slams the window frame down onto my fingers.

– Keep Your Sisters Close & Your Enemies Closer –

The chapel door creeps open. Standing beneath its archway is Father Parfitt, dressed in white, his torch trained on my face. The light blinds me for a moment, so I hold up an arm to shield my eyes.

His footsteps strike the stone floor, each one closer than the last. He gets within a few feet of me before he kills the switch and rests the torch on a wooden pew in the front row. He takes another step closer, placing his leather bible down on the altar. Then finally he stops, his face no more than half a pace from mine.

A brisk wind blows through the crack beneath the window, running up my spine.

But Father Parfitt doesn't flinch.

'It's not what you think,' I say. 'I'm not one of them. But I know who they are. I can lead you to them, if you want. Just spare my sister Scarlett. I beg you.'

Parfitt's heavily lined face doesn't even move. His deep-set eyes just glare at me, staring right through me. Then he raises his hand and reaches towards my chest. I try to push it away, but even though we're standing right next to one another, somehow I miss.

His arm keeps coming. Then it passes right through me and pulls on the sash window behind, forcing it shut. A nauseous feeling swirls in my stomach, as if someone has just reached inside and touched my soul.

I watch as Parfitt turns around and starts to walk away. He takes the torch from the front row and tries to turn it on. At first it doesn't work, but then he strikes it into the palm of his hand and the little bulb lights up.

'Oh, I almost forgot,' he says, turning back towards me.

Then he takes his bible from the altar and heads back down the aisle. He fumbles for a moment, tucking the thick book under his arm, so he can turn the door handle. A single page falls to the floor, but he doesn't seem to notice. Without looking back, he disappears through the door and I hear it being locked behind him.

My head spins, still unsure of what has actually happened. I run to the door and pick up the loose page. The moment I touch it, I realise what it is. It's not rough like paper. It's smooth and cold like the pages of Emily's book.

I squint, frantically trying to read it in the darkness, but it seems there is only one line of writing.

To those we trust to keep us safe.

It makes no sense at all. But then I turn it over. Suddenly I realise what I'm looking at. Written at the very top is the name Emily Whitehurst. It's Emily's story. I'd noticed a few pages were missing when I was reading about Alice yesterday.

But what the hell is Parfitt doing, carrying Emily's page around?

At that moment there's a deep rumbling from the floor. The stone tablet that Emily said was the gateway to hell begins to rise upwards. There's a loud grating noise as it scrapes across the stone floor to reveal an opening and a set of steps.

I stuff the loose page in my back pocket and watch, hearing voices echo beneath me.

The first thing I see is Emily's fire-red hair. She's clutching her book in one hand and a candle in the other. The twins appear next, each with a candle too. But they're also leading two teenage girls in front of them, both of whom appear to be sleepwalking.

Then Alice comes up the stairs, escorting an older woman of large build. They're followed by Paige and another girl in a trance. They all congregate in the aisle in the very centre of the chapel, making just enough room for Hope, who is leading a sleeping toddler by the hand.

'What's going on?' I say.

'Where do you want me to begin?' Emily says, edging towards me.

'You've opened the gateway,' I say. 'And they're the missing girls, aren't they?'

Emily starts to laugh wildly and then the others join in.

'Oh, Rose, how foolish you've been.' Emily pauses. 'Or should I say Scarlett-Rose.'

'I don't know what you mean,' I say. 'My name is Rose. My sister's name is Scarlett.'

'Sister?' Emily says. 'You thought I was your sister a moment ago. The truth is you don't know what it means to be a sister. And now you'll never know what it means.'

'I know that Scarlett is my sister,' I insist. 'And I know that even though she drives me crazy sometimes, I'd do anything to save her.'

'You have *such* strong feelings for her,' Emily says. 'Such sweet memories of the two of you growing up together. Although you were always in the background, weren't you, Rose?'

'So what?' I say. 'At least she'd never double-cross me.'

'No,' says Emily, her green eyes almost glowing in the dark. 'The reason you were always in the background is because you are not Scarlett's sister. Your full name is Scarlett-Rose. Your body lies in the hospital, whilst your spirit stands here in front of us. It was brought through by Jack, your boyfriend, less than a week ago.'

I try to shut out her voice, but it's hopeless.

'You are the gateway, Scarlett-Rose,' Emily says.

I try to deny it, but I can't. Suddenly it all makes sense. The memories of always being in Scarlett's shadow. The conversations I had with Jack over the past week…

'It's not like that,' he says, pulling out a set of keys and a battered orange helmet from his bag. 'It's just

with all that's happening right now, I can't be dealing
with ghosts as well.'

'I'm just not ready for this,' he says. 'I'm not ready
to say goodbye.'

Then there's the kiss. And Mum ignoring me. Her
strange behaviour in the bathroom. Her going on about
the letter I left for her on the kitchen table. I nearly
kicked the door off its hinges; no wonder she looked
like she was having a nervous breakdown.

'You know I'm right, don't you?' Emily says,
slowly walking towards me. 'But guess what? All those
memories are going to fade away at any moment.'

'I don't understand,' I say, as the others begin to
follow her. 'What do you mean?'

'You are the gateway,' Emily says. 'A spirit not
attached to their own body. On this night, Halloween
night, we are going to use you as a vehicle back into
this world. We'll each steal a body for our own. We'll
swap souls with these five girls here. Then we'll
reappear in Burnham All-Saints and nobody will even
know.'

'And what about you?' I say, already knowing the
answer. 'Whose body will you steal?'

'I'll have yours. I'll wake up in that hospital bed,
just before sunrise.'

I see the twins step out from behind Emily. I'm
completely surrounded.

'Wait a minute,' I say. 'If Jack brought me through and we woke up the others by using the book, how did you get here, Emily?'

'My page was already returned to the place of my death,' Emily laughs, the candle she's holding lighting up her face. 'The stupid preacher man carries it around with him, like some badge of honour to the witch-finding club. The clumsy old codger must have dropped it on just about every inch of this abbey, at one time or another. Truth be told, old Gideon wouldn't know a witch if she walked right up to him with a candle in her hand.'

'No,' I say. 'But I might!'

I pull Emily's page from my pocket and thrust it into the flame of her candle. Emily's bright red hair begins to smoke. Then it begins to smoulder. Within seconds she bursts into flames, dropping the book of human skin in front of her.

The rest of them pause for a moment. I watch their faces fall into shock. Emily screams out in pain. Her whole body is engulfed in flames and her arms flap wildly, trying to extinguish the fire.

Madelyn buries her head between her hands. I see hesitation in Evelyn's eyes – they're torn between helping Emily and making a grab for the book. I gaze back at Paige, Alice and even little Hope. I look at the girls standing before them, all in a trance, blissfully unaware of the danger they're in.

Then I kick the book of human skin towards Emily's burning body.

The twins burst into the flames, followed by Alice and Paige. Fire begins to lick its way across the red oak pews and starts to devour the whole room. Thick smoke curls up to the rafters, making it hard to see who is who.

Every nerve in my body tells me I need to get out of there. But I can't leave the other girls. With my arms held out in front of me, I fumble through the dense smoke, the witches dancing all around me in agony.

I find the sleeping girls. Opening my arms as wide as I can, I shield them from the blaze. The flames gnaw away at my skin; the heat is almost unbearable and the air is too thick to breathe.

Then I scream at the top of my voice. 'I channel the Earth in the name of my sisters. Air, soil, water and fire, let my sisters wake.'

My lungs begin to fill with smoke. With flames closing in all around me, I hang on a little longer. Bending low with pain, I catch sight of little Hope clinging to my leg, her body yet to be set alight. With my last fragments of strength, I lift her up to my chest, holding her tightly.

'Sorores in Aeternum!' I scream.

The next thing I know my eyes are flashing open. At first my vision is blurred. Then I see two figures in white, like angels, looming towards me. Their presence makes me feel uneasy, as if they're about to take me away.

216

I look up.

Light burns above them, shading their faces and drawing me towards it.

An incessant beeping buzzes all around me. A large tube runs from my mouth and a number of wires tether me to the bed, stopping me disappearing into the light.

The beeping gets faster.

The figures in white come into focus.

One is a doctor, I can tell by the stethoscope hanging from his neck. And the other is the familiar face of Father Parfitt.

'Wait a second,' the doctor says. 'Something is happening.'

Suddenly a crowd of nurses rush to my bedside. Then, through the crowd, I see Mum. Her greasy hair hasn't been washed in a month and her eyes are so bloodshot, they look like they've cried themselves dry.

'Scarlett,' she says. 'My Scarlett-Rose, can you hear me?'

I pull the oxygen mask away from my face. 'Mum? Is that you?'

'Of course it's me,' she says, tears streaming down her face. 'Don't speak. In fact, don't move. You've been in a terrible accident. I thought you were dead.'

'Not dead,' I say, my voice cracking. 'Just sleeping.'

'I said don't speak,' Mum says, as the doctor pushes her aside.

'I need everybody to step back,' he orders. 'Give her some air.'

'I'm fine,' I say, sitting upright. 'Where's Jack? I want to see him.'

I catch sight of his spiked hair, poking up beyond the crowd. One by one the doctor and the nurses step aside, so only Jack and Mum are left at my bedside.

'What did I tell you?' I say.

'You told me to make them wait, just in case you were late,' Jack says.

'And was I?' I say.

'No,' Jack says. 'You were just on time.'

The doctor asks Mum and Jack to leave for a while, so that he can run some tests. I feel him take some blood from my arm and a nurse comes in to adjust my pillows. But before long, I find myself drifting back off to sleep.

I'm still a little drowsy when I overhear the doctor talking to Father Parfitt by my bed. 'Well, Father,' he says. 'It's a terrible shame about the fire last night, but I make it three miracles in one day.'

'Three?' asks Father Parfitt.

'Yes,' the doctor replies. 'The missing girls found in the abbey, Scarlett-Rose waking up, and now I just got the results of her blood tests. You're not going to believe this.'

'Try me,' Father Parfitt says. 'I know that the Lord works in mysterious ways.'

'Well, somehow young Scarlett-Rose is pregnant,' the doctor says. 'We need to do a scan, but provisionally, it seems that both mum and baby are going to be fine.'

– Other Books From Daniel Adkins –

One Thousand White Whales

This fantasy adventure is aimed at the whole family and will appeal to anyone with a childlike imagination and a love for planet Earth. When a dark change sweeps across his homeland, ten year-old Nanuk is sent on a journey to the North Pole. As he attempts to cross an entire continent on foot, the Northern Lights do more than guide him - they teach him the deepest, darkest secrets of the entire universe

Lines of Liberty

With an iconic setting, this psychological thriller is for an adult only audience. Eloise is the envy of all her friends when she is sent on a business trip to Venice. First class tickets on British Airways and a room at the Hilton with an amazing view across the blue-green waters of the Adriatic. But within twenty-four hours, she finds herself drawn into a world of sex, lies and murder, unable to escape until she works out the identity of a dark mysterious stranger.

To find out more, please visit…

WWW.Daniel Adkins Secret Bookshelf .Com

– Why not post a review on Facebook? –

As a reader myself, the most common reason for me choosing a book is that somebody I know has recommended it. So why not post a review of Sleeping Sisters on facebook. Tell people what you liked about it and be sure to tell them where they can get hold of a copy. Sleeping Sisters is available on the internet via Amazon and feedaread and it can also be ordered through large bookshops on the High Street. But the best place to discover more about my writing is through my website, where you can follow me on social media and read free samples before you buy.

WWW.Daniel Adkins Secret Bookshelf .Com

Lightning Source UK Ltd.
Milton Keynes UK
UKOW03f1955130814

236899UK00001B/7/P